FERRIS' HOUSE

OYSTERBACK
HARDSHELL
METHODIST
CHURCH

The Oysterback Tales

Powerlines over Oysterback Creek

THE

OYSTERBACK TALES

Helen Chappell

THE JOHNS HOPKINS UNIVERSITY PRESS
BALTIMORE AND LONDON

The Johns Hopkins University Press
2715 North Charles Street
Baltimore, Maryland 21218-4319
The Johns Hopkins Press Ltd., London

Library of Congress Cataloging-in-Publication Data

Chappell, Helen, 1947–
    The Oysterback tales / Helen Chappell ; with a foreword by
Harold D. Piper ; illustrations by the author.
        p.   cm.
    ISBN 0-8018-4815-6 (acid-free). — ISBN 0-8018-4816-4 (pbk. :
acid-free)
    1. City and town life—Eastern Shore (Md. and Va.)—Fiction.
I. Title.
PS3553.H299097   1994
813'.54—dc20   93-37407

A catalog record of this book is available from the British Library.

Portions of this book have appeared, in slightly altered form, in
the Baltimore Sun.

Contents

Foreword

Oysterback began with the thud of a sandbag dropped on my groin. Like the pith-helmeted Sir Richard Burton seeking the source of the Nile, green-smocked surgeons had worked back through my arteries and discovered that, contrary to some unkind opinions, I have a heart. Thus reassured, I had only to lie motionless for ten hours while the sandbag's weight sealed up my artery. One of Helen Chappell's novels beguiled the time.

The novel was not about Oysterback, which had yet to be invented, but it led to my making a phone call to Helen when I got out from under the sandbag. I proposed that she write an occasional piece of local color about Maryland's Eastern Shore for the Opinion • Commentary page of the *Baltimore Sun*. No features about decoy carvers or antique shoppes, I begged; give me articles that convey a sense of place and life. So Helen created Oysterback. In spite of my strictures, we have decoy carvers and antique shoppes but, freed of the burden of fact, they come imbedded in a wonderful "found" world.

Helen's achievement is not unique, I suppose. One thinks of Faulkner's Yoknapatawpha County, of Al Capp's Dogpatch—authentic communities with shared memories, folklore, feuds, pleasures, and humiliations. But those creators had space—long novels, a comic strip that ran for years—in which to build up characters and situations. "Oysterback Tales" gets only one 800–1,000 word shot a month, because it is my belief (although perhaps not Helen's) that more frequent exposure might spoil a good thing. That one article must be self-contained, with all the necessary exposition camouflaged in plot and dialogue, because newspaper readers can't be expected to remember from one month to the next that Miss Nettie is Hudson Swann's mother-in-law and Hagar Jump is both Oysterback's postmaster and its leading thespian. (Perhaps it's the other way around; Helen hasn't sent this month's column yet.)

Believe it or not, some Eastern Shore folk take offense at some of the

Oysterback characterizations.* I get complaints now and then that "Helen is making fun of us." I always remind the callers that Oysterback's denizens are ridiculous, completely unlike real Eastern Shore people. Of course, I'm being disingenuous. Eastern Shore people are exactly as ridiculous and as lovable as Oysterback people, Western Shore people, and everybody else.

Helen's success with Oysterback doesn't rely on just getting the accent right or taking us to fabulous events like the transvestite beauty pageant down to the volunteer fire department. If that were all, "Oysterback Tales" would indeed be simply a column that makes fun of Eastern Shore people, and it would have lost its novelty and its readership long ago. Instead, it has grown as readers find delight in the telling detail (a teenaged "mall rat" encountered in a movie theater) and the wacky invention (a mold spot, shaped like Elvis, around which Desiree Grinch is building a shrine).

Most of all, readers take delight in the recognition of themselves and their own absurdities. For we all live in Oysterbacks of our own, surrounded by odd folks whom we take for granted. My barber, I think, must have gotten her early training in Doreen Redmond's Curl Up 'n' Dye Salon de Beaute. My environmentalist neighbor is surely a long-lost brother of the strange and moody Ferrus T. Buckett. And there's even a little bit of me, of all people, in Desiree Grinch (of all people)—although I suspect there's a bit more of Helen in her.

Where is Oysterback? Well, it's over the rainbow and down Tobacco Road, somewhere between Brigadoon and Shangri-La. And it's over the fence and down the block, somewhere between the mall and suburbia. Enjoy your visit. Pick up a copy of the *Bugeye* to keep up with the social notes. And be sure to drop by the Blue Crab Tavern (prop., Desiree Grinch) for fine refreshments and stimulating companionship.

Harold D. Piper
Editor, Opinion • Commentary
Baltimore Sun

---

*Some Eastern Shore folk take offense at *anything*. Talbot County, for instance, is famous for having absolutely no sense of humor about itself. Or anything else.—H.C.

Honorary Citizens of Oysterback

Hal Piper, my *Baltimore Sun* editor, has his own house on Log Cabin Point. Michel Pratka is welcome any time; at JHUP, in order of appearance, Jack Goellner, Arlene Sullivan, Bob Brugger, and all the other great folks who helped put this book together, especially Jeanne Pinault, my copyeditor. On the Home Front: Randolph Murphy, aka The Prince of Tilghman Island, Edwina and Dan Murphy, Rick Kollinger, Bill Horne, and The Boys down to the West Side and over to Tilghman. At *Chesapeake Bay*, Jean Waller, Barbara Goyette, and Starke Jett. This book was made possible by a grant from the Dotti Heimert Foundation for Wayward Writers and the support of Captain L. E. Chappell Jr.

You all are always welcome in Oysterback; you can pick up Oysters Desiree and your keys to the city down to the Blue Crab any Wednesday night.

The Oysterback Tales

From Professor Shepherd's *History of Oysterback*

On the Widgeon Marsh Causeway from Wallopsville, you will come to the town of Oysterback, which lies on high ground in the middle of Great Santimoke Marsh at the mouth of the Devanaux River. Oysterback was named for the oystershell midden on which the town was built. According to Native American legend, its original name (now lost) meant the Dwelling Place of Misty, Spirit of Planked Shad. The village was settled in the mid-1600s by runaway indentured servants, escaped slaves, accused witches, and outcast Native Americans from the Santimoke Confederacy. This varied assortment of political and religious pariahs prized its marshy isolation and the fact that no one else much wanted the place.

Universal suffrage seems to have been *de facto* from the inception of the town. In early records, Fauntleroy Calvert, appointed overseer of the West Hundred by relatives in London, described the Oysterback population as "Heathen pyrates, wytches, watermenne and Dissenters of ev'ry Persuasion, Sexxe and colore who declaire themselves to answer to No Authoritie save ye Lord Godde Jehovah and theyre own Zoning Boarde." He suggested mounting an armed expedition to wipe out these dangerous radicals, but London, occupied at the time with the bubonic plague and the Great Fire, never responded, and Fauntleroy, who married Longsuffering Baldwin, daughter of the planter Odor-of-Sanctity Baldwin of Gloom Hill, contented himself with building the singularly ugly brick manor at Mount Boredom (open M–Tu–W, 10–4; restored in 1954 by the West Hundred Historical Society).

Oysterback retained its reputation for tough-minded independence and occasional piracy until the Revolutionary War, when several Hessians, having lost their way during the Battle of Pinworm Point, stumbled into town with some month-old broadsheets, accidentally rallying the population to a winning cause.

The Hessian conscripts, liking Oysterback, started the first brewery on the Eastern Shore on the site of what is now Doreen's Curl Up 'n' Dye Salon de Beaute. (Historical Marker 4012.) Auld Elektor's Jungenbrau, a local favorite for nearly a century, was said to owe its taste to the use of tuckahoe flavoring in the barley mash. The brewery building collapsed during Hurricane Wanda in 1952.

Thomas Jefferson blew into Oysterback by mistake during a stormy trip across the Chesapeake. He described his visit in a letter to Maria Cosway. "Although rec'd. with warm hospitality, good crabcakes and beer . . . I cd. not shake the sensation that I was a visitor to another, albeit *greatly democratic,* planet." The third president's remarks, certainly meant in jest, may have led to the local belief that Oysterback was founded by settlers from the planet Uranus, an idea that persists in Santimoke County to this writing.

It was not to be expected that Oysterback would escape the Great Awakening led by Joshua Thomas, the Parson of the Islands. As with other watermen's communities on the Shore, the town embraced Methodism with fervor about the time of the War of 1812.

Characteristically, Oysterback eventually chose to go its own way. Oysterback Hardshell Methodist Church (ca. 1826) broke from the West Hundred Charge over the "God is a Waterman" Doctrine of 1857. "The story that baseball is an organized religion in Oysterback is not true," says local historian Ferrus T. Buckett, "but a good World Series, that's another thing."

Distracted by the enormous amount of paperwork caused by the War Between the States, Abraham Lincoln lost the Declaration of Secession sent to him by Oysterback, which, disgusted with events, voted to detach itself from Maryland, the United States, and the Confederacy.

In the 1880s oyster boom, Oysterback had a renowned skipjack fleet. Alas, most of it sank in a territorial dispute with the rival fleet from Wingo, Virginia. The pilings of Long Wharf, where the steamboat *Millard Fillmore* and the floating theater *John Wilkes Booth* once put in, are still visible at Log Cabin Point.

Local legend has it there was a game warden around Oysterback during the Great Depression, but no one seems to know what happened to him; the more recent and highly publicized disappearance of powerful wetlands real estate developer J. Snidely Grubb also remains a mystery.

Today, Oysterback is best known for its Mosquito Festival, which attracts *Culex pipiens* lovers from three continents (second weekend in August, call 410/555-5678 for details), and as the hometown of Orioles outfielder Hooley Legume, lauded by Cal Ripken with "Well, if they traded Legume, they might get someone worse. Y'know?"

The Silver Cord Is Broken, the Golden Bowl Is Loose: Read All about It in the *Oysterback Bugeye*

TWO HEARTS BEAT AS ONE last week when Jeanne Leery married Hudson Swann at Oysterback Hardshell Methodist Church in a double-ring ceremony. The bride sang her own selections, including "Oh, Promise Me," "We've Only Just Begun," and "I'd Rather Have Jesus." The bride is a popular local beauty operator at Doreen's Curl Up 'n' Dye Salon de Beaute, and the groom is a self-employed waterman.

• • •

HAGAR JUMP, OYSTERBACK'S POSTMASTER, says that the new catalogs from the Farm and Tractor Store have arrived and will be put up this week. Incidentally, Ray Bob Whortley and Sudie Fairbank, your box rents are due.

• • •

PARSONS DREEDLE OF DREEDLE'S FUNERAL HOME wants everyone to know that the butterbeans they offer at their roadside produce stand are not red because they fertilize them with funeral wastes, as some have been saying, but because they come from the seed company like that and grow that way naturally. This should relieve many minds in the local area.

• • •

BOOT WILLIS REPORTS that he has tonged up an oyster that is the size of a size 13 Redball boot. Those who wish to view the giant bivalve may do so by stopping by the Blue Crab Tavern, where it is on display inside of Boot's Coleman chest over by the Pac Man machine. Better hurry, because Blue Crab Proprietor Desiree Grinch is running a special on her popular Oysters Desiree this weekend.

• • •

LOCAL ARTIST AND EDITOR of this newspaper Helga Wallop, whose paintings on velvet of small children, clowns, and Elvis have been exhibited as far away as the First Bank of Delaware in Dover, will be giving a Kristmas Krafts Workshop at the Community Center on the 9th. Those interested in making a beautiful and original Christmas

3

wreath, bring a one-gallon Clorox container, two pairs of pantyhose, and a blowtorch.

• • •

CAPTAIN AND MRS. LENNIE SKINNER are enjoying a visit from Mrs. Skinner's cousins, Captain and Mrs. Elwood Rainbird, and family at their rental cottage in Ocean City this week. "Old Timers" will remember Mrs. Rainbird as the former Juanita Bugg, Delmarva Poultry Princess of 1948.

THE SILVER CORD IS BROKEN, the golden bowl is loose as friends of Haney Sparks are invited to call at Dreedle's Funeral Home on Wednesday night for a last look at the departed. Haney Sparks, universally known throughout the Delmarva region, was called to his eternal rest after eating his usual nacho cheese steak sandwich snack in front of Omar Hinton's store the other day. Omar wants all West Hundred watermen to know that the back-ordered supply of zinc weights have finally come in just in time for crab pot building.

• • •

SHERIFF WESLEY BRISCOE issued a citation to Huddie Swann and Junior Redmond for driving their motorized Port-O-San duck blind down Black Dog Road last week without registration.

• • •

FARADAY HICKS'S DAUGHTER LA VERNE and her husband Bubba are visiting him from New Carrollton as they do every time he says he's leaving all his money to Tammy Faye Bakker.

• • •

MR. EDDIE, POPULAR HAIRDRESSER down to Doreen's Curl Up 'n' Dye and Director of Patamoke Community Theatre, reports that Hagar Jump, Oysterback's postmaster, will be playing Mary again this year in the Drive In Christmas Pageant. Let us hope that proper reverence will be shown this year and that the Three Wise Men will not appear in their VFD fire gear saying they have "come from a fahr."

• • •

ALONZO DEAVER is resting quietly at home after spending four of a possible six months on probation before judgment at the Santimoke County Detention Center. Those who wish to visit or recover their missing property are asked to call in the evenings.

• • •

REVEREND CLAUDE CROUCH brought his Currency for Christ Crusade to Wallopsville last week, featuring the Boudine Family, the snake handling gospel quartet. Special guests included Miss Jean Fitts from Animal Control. When Rev. Crouch asked Ferrus T. Buckett if he had found Jesus, Ferrus said he didn't know He was lost.

• • •

FRIENDS OF JUNIOR AND DOREEN REDMOND helped celebrate their 8th anniversary down to the Blue Crab last week. The couple's four children and two Labs were present to add to the fun. Doreen and Junior say the money tree will help them with their second honeymoon at Capt. and Mrs. Lennie Skinner's rental cottage at Ocean City. Entertainment included Tonto Snavely, the Elvis-impersonating waterman from Patamoke, as well as Poot Wallop's imitation of Tonto imitating Elvis.

• • •

MRS. ANTOINETTE "NETTIE" LEERY won the Jello Mold-Off Contest down to the Wallopsville Community Center again this year with her secret Harlequin Pecan Cool Whip Dream recipe.

• • •

THAT BIG FRACAS LAST WEEK was not, as reported here earlier, the work of outsiders from the planet Uranus, but the work of Junior "Junie" Redmond and the boys over to the Blue Crab Tavern and Assistant Deputy Sheriff Johnny Ray Insley, although he didn't know it at the time. Junie says it was supposed to be a practical joke and that he will pay all the damages on Mrs. Carlotta Hackett's 1963 pink Cadillac, repair the hole in the P.O. door, and remove all the paint from Faraday

Hicks's cows. No damage was sustained to the seafood plant, the work-boat, the dogs, or the fire tower.

• • •

MRS. CARLOTTA HACKETT'S VISIT to Louisa "Sister" Gibbs over to Patamoke was abruptly cut short when she was operated on for a 7-pound tumor in the shape of Richard Nixon. Pix of Carlotta and tumor appear on page 3.

•

Bargain Day over to Omar's Store

It's amazing how rumors get started. Like what happened last Saturday when Earl Don and I were on our way to his parents' fortieth anniversary party over to Wallopsville. Now, if some people in this town have nothing better to do than hang around Omar Hinton's store and listen to other peoples' business, that's their problem, and they need a life. This community has lots of opportunities to do volunteer work, for one thing.

I, Desiree Grinch, proprietor of the Blue Crab Tavern, have a life, and believe me, it keeps me busy enough minding my own business without looking into everyone else's, like some.

Anyway, if anyone really needs to know, that's what I was doing over to Omar Hinton's store last Saturday, teetering on my stiletto heels, with Earl Don in the truck leaning on the horn and screaming about us being a half-hour late to the party to start with. He just wanted to get that necktie off. No one hates wearing a tie quite as much as Earl Don. It was not, as some people around here have been saying, another one of our domestic disputes.

See, I thought Earl Don bought a present and he thought I bought a present so what happened was no one bought a present, even though Earl Don was past the Farm and Tractor Store over to Salisbury three times last week, and I haven't been able to get out from behind the bar for a month, what with waiting for the cable TV people. Your basic lost cause, those cable TV boys, but I digress.

You know I like Omar Hinton; most people do. He is a nice man and has made a fine president of the Oysterback town council. Why, he never even turned an eyelash when we woke him up at 3 a.m. when Earl Don and I were babysitting little Olivier and ran out of Pampers. That takes some niceness.

But even I will have to admit that Omar is a pack rat, plain and simple. He has a lot of trouble throwing anything out, as anyone who has spent any time poking around in the back of his store can tell you. Since I enjoy poking around back there, I know for a fact that there's stuff back there that's been there since his grandfather's time. Even Omar doesn't know what he's got back there. But I do.

7

"Omar, I need an anniversary present, quick!" I says.

"This store is all right if you are planning to give someone a can of Indian Quarter Cream Corn, a pack of Peanut Butter Tandy Cakes, or a small bottle of Janitor In a Drum, but you are talking relatives of yours here, people you've eaten crabs with," Omar says, with his eyebrows all the way where his hair used to be.

"I'll find something," I says, heading for the back room.

"Mebbe you was thinkin' of matchin' Barlow knives?" Omar calls. I must say, he manages to amuse himself sometimes.

But I was already rooting around behind the patent medicine and the other stuff Omar has up there behind the old ice cream freezer, where no one ever looks. "If you spent as much time dusting your stock as you do playing checkers, you'd be a good storekeeper, Omar," I says to him, sort of teasing. I knew the odds were with me, that I would find something back there.

And there it was, where it had been since he'd moved it in 1961 to make way for the Red Ball boot display. A dusty Wallopsville Church Centennial Commemorative Plate, dated 1958. The perfect collectible for Earl Don's folks' collection. At the original price.

"Here's what I want," I says. "Sticker says 39 cents."

Omar sort of pursed up his lips, and I knew what he was thinking. But he rang it up. I ended up spending more money on gift wrap than the gift, which I wrapped up while Earl Don was taking the corners on two wheels, yelling at me because we were late. As it was, we barely made the minister's invocation.

Earl Don's folks were thrilled with their Wallopsville Church plate, which I understand costs a fortune in antique stores.

Don't believe everything you hear over to Omar Hinton's store. That, my friends, is what really happened.

Ferrus T. Buckett Deals with Hard Times

I t was one of those days that winter hands out every once in a while, with a sudden break in the cold and a gentle southerly breeze that hints of spring to come.

Down at the end of Black Dog Road, Ferrus T. Buckett rocked back and forth in his creaky chair, sucking on his dentures as he read the latest issue of *Paris-Match* in the warm sunlight. At his feet, Blackie, his ancient and half-senile Lab, pricked up his ears at the sound of an approaching car.

Ferrus barely glanced up as the glossy new Mercedes, painted an eye-blinding white, roared past, then suddenly stopped in a flurry of brake lights and squealing tires. After a moment, it began to slowly back up until it was parallel with Ferrus' littered wonder of an overgrown yard, decorated with all matter of rusting engine parts and extinct appliances. A woman's face, disapproving and haughty, floated in the smoked glass of the passenger's window, peering at Ferrus as if he were a particularly unappealing insect.

"Well, offer him a little money, for God's sake," Ferrus heard her voice, thick with the accents of the Western Shore, through the open sunroof. "Obviously he's just some old cracker trash. He has no idea what it's really worth."

It would be a Lem Ward, Muffy. None of these people know the value of anything," her male companion said. "Now, I know my decoys. You just watch me."

A man climbed out of the passenger seat. Like the car, everything about him was too new and too expensive.

The man strode into the yard without so much as a by-your-leave and picked up an ancient decoy carelessly resting against an old deep freezer lid. He turned it this way and that, tapped it with his finger, and even sniffed it like a wine cork. Apparently satisfied, he walked a few feet deeper into the yard. "I say, Pops, this decoy is quite interesting. A bufflehead, isn't it? I collect decoys, don't you know."

"Is that right," Ferrus replied. With his old man's fingers, he carefully creased his place in *Paris-Match*.

"Oh yes," the man continued. "Know everything there is to know about them. This is rather an interesting specimen, don't you know. Not terribly valuable, I daresay, but interesting."

"Is that right," Ferrus said again. He took out his pipe and began to fill it from his pouch, carefully tamping the sweet-smelling tobacco into the bowl. "Been around here forever. Gave up gunnin' when my joints got too bad to move. 'At 'ere ole 'coy ain't no good for gunnin' no more. Liefer not use a string that old; she'd heave up on you."

Ferrus was reminded of the churchy caution against avarice as he watched expressions flickering across the man's face. Nothing could be read in his own countenance, however.

The woman was tapping on the car window, mouthing something at her companion.

"Well, listen, old man," the Mercedes owner said impatiently. "What do you say to selling this old thing to me? Give you fifty."

"They got a whole goddam museum over to town fulla them ole 'coys," Ferrus said.

If looks could kill, Ferrus would have been dead on the rotten planking.

"Gerald, pay the man and let's get out of Tobacco Road. I would really, really like to be at Fager's by four." The woman leaned out the window now. With her blonde hair skimmed back from her head, she looked like a made-up skull.

"Take a hunnert," Ferrus said matter-of-factly.

The Mercedes man had trouble holding the decoy and pulling a thick roll of bills from his pants pocket at the same time. He handed Ferrus a bill, tendered between his second and third fingers, as if touch with the old waterman could contaminate him.

Ferrus was still tucking the bill in his shirt pocket when the glimmering Mercedes did a U-turn and headed down the road.

"I'm so sure that it's a Ward!" The woman's voice hung in the air.

As soon as they were out of sight, Ferrus got up and walked around the back yard. Taking up his shovel, he began to dig in the manure pile, exposing a beautifully if artificially aged, wooden snow goose. "Oh, I'm so sure that it's a Ward!" he muttered in imitation of the woman's nasal accents. He began to chuckle. "Not," he added, bearing the goose proudly to the front yard.

Hudson Swann Eludes the Law

T hings have been pretty quiet in Oysterback of late. Not so much as a knee-deep's peep, as Altus Rycker likes to say, except he says something different. It's sort of a relief after all the excitement we had last week, what with Huddie and the Beauty and the Beast Contest down at the fire hall and Miss Nettie Leery and all.

I guess you know what a Beauty and the Beast is. It's when they can find five or six boys on the Fire Department who will dress up like women—makeup, wigs, and all—and become contestants in a beauty contest. It's always popular, and it always raises a lot of money for the Fire Department, as there is nothing people like more than to see grown men make fools out of themselves.

They run it just like a beauty contest for women—evening gown, swimsuit, and talent competition. Of course, it gets pretty raunchy sometimes, but you should see the little old ladies, right up in front, where butter wouldn't melt in their mouths, watching those boys with their chests all stuffed out and all that makeup smeared all over their beards and mustaches, hairy legs just hangin' out of their skirts and women's maillots and what-not, big feet stuck into high-heeled shoes.

Oh, it is funny, I have to admit, especially when Junie Redmond emcees it. When the boys forget their lines, he just jumps right in and covers up for them like a real actor or something.

Well, Hudson Swann swore up and down they'd never get him into one of those outfits and up on that stage, but somehow or another Junie convinced him to do it this year.

Well, Jeanne, Hudson's wife, being a beauty operator, had a wig and makeup and all of that, but she's a tiny little thing and Huddie's over six foot, so she told him to go into town and buy himself some sort of evening gown from the thrift shop at the hospital.

So, Huddie went on into town, but when he got to the thrift shop, it was run by these genteel little old ladies, all of them friends of his mother, Miss Catherine, and Huddie, who is by nature not a talker to start, found that he just couldn't tell the ladies that he needed a dress for himself but he didn't know what size he wore. He was just too embarrassed. Now Junior Redmond would have done it, but not Huddie; they're best friends, but they're as opposite as night and day. So, Huddie stole out, dressless, and went to Dave's Sport Shop to console himself with some new Spin Doctor Da-Glos.

He was standing there looking at the moosehead Dave keeps hanging over the counter when he all of a sudden got this idea, or so he says. Huddie's mother-in-law, Miss Nettie Leery, is quite a big woman, and maybe she would have a gown that would fit him. Huddie gets ideas like that.

So, Miss Nettie was over in Log Cabin Point that day visiting her sister, so Huddie just went over to her cedar closet. Miss Nettie wouldn't attend any Beauty and the Beast Contest on a dare, so Huddie figured if he could get it in and out of her house without her knowing it, he'd be home free. What he found was this pink lace number, and he just sort of looped it over his arm and took it on down to the VFD, so it would be

there that night when he came to get all dressed up for the contest.

So, when he gets there after supper and sees that all the other boys have gone to considerable trouble with shoes and nylons and hats and all, and these are big macho guys we're talking about, Huddie sees he's gonna need a little something special. So, after a couple pitchers of beer, he decides that the pink plastic flamingoes in front of the trailer home of Miss Hagar Jump, Oysterback's postmaster, would make a nice hat. So, in his pink lace dress and his high heels and his wig and makeup, Huddie goes down the street and sort of borrows Miss Hagar's flamingoes.

Trouble is, Miss Hagar looks out the window and sees this big woman in this pink lace dress stealing her flamingoes, and she calls Johnny Ray Insley, the deputy sheriff.

So, Hudson enters the contest with this hat made out of these pink plastic flamingoes, and well, you know how these things go, what with the gown and the talent and the swimsuit competition, Huddie is second runner-up. Huddie is also very glad that it's all over. You never saw a man put his own clothes back on so fast in your whole life.

First thing in the morning, he returns his mother-in-law's dress, and just as he's coming down the back stairs, he hears Miss Nettie turning in the drive. So, Huddie just has time to make it out the back door. But he forgets the flamingoes and leaves them in Miss Nettie's washroom, on top of the dryer.

Wouldn't you know, Miss Nettie's going to the Overstreet girl's wedding that very afternoon, and she's wearing that pink lace dress.

Well, who else should be going to Miss Overstreet's wedding but Miss Hagar Jump? And who's been feuding over who won first prize in the tomato jelly contest at the Flower and Garden Show last year but Miss Hagar and Miss Nettie?

Well, Miss Hagar takes one look, and I mean one look at Miss Nettie in that pink lace dress, and jumps up right there in church and calls Johnny Ray Insley.

Well, Johnny Ray didn't want to do it, but Hagar fussed and took on so that Johnny Ray went on over to Miss Nettie's house. Miss Nettie was indignant; she said go right ahead and look, and of course there were those two pink plastic flamingoes right there in her washroom.

Don't you know Miss Hagar tried to press charges? And Nettie actually had to go over to the sheriff's office until Jeanne and Hudson came over and straightened everything out.

Well, Jeanne took on; after all, Miss Nettie is her mother, but poor ole Hudson didn't know which way to look. Everything he said or did was wrong.

In the end they straightened it all out, of course, but poor Huddie. That's why he's been living on board his boat lately.

He says at least he has his second runner-up trophy for company, if he doesn't drink it first.

How Ferrus T. Buckett Foretold the Oscars

E veryone around here knows Ferrus T. Buckett. About three or four years ago, they sent somebody down from the *Sun* up to Baltimore to interview him for being the world's oldest waterman, which of course we already knew. Ferrus T. Buckett is somewhere between about a hundred-eighty and death, although Miss Nettie Leery, who writes the Oysterback Socials for the *Bugeye,* says he was in the same class back to the one-room school with her father, which makes him about 93.

Ferrus T. Buckett lives down at the end of Black Dog Road in this little house, over the marsh. There's all kinds of really neat stuff around his place, like old freezers and pieces of old Ford pickups scattered all over the place, but even when we were kids, we never went down there and took anything, not even when Huddie Swann needed a rod for that '51 Ford he used to run up and down the roads back in high school. We all knew that Ferrus would just as soon shoot a trespasser with that .30-.30 as a squirrel. Probably eat trespasser for dinner, too.

Hagar Jump, the postmaster, says he turned sullen when his wife died. Ain't no kids that anyone knows of, just Ferrus T. and those old Labs of his that would bite you as easy as look at you. He's all wrinkled up and weatherbeaten, but he's strong.

The thing is, you can set your calendar by Ferrus T. Buckett. When he goes to setting out his eel pots, you know the last snow has fallen and spring's coming. Oh, he still works the water, all right; eels all spring, runs his trotlines all summer, and tongs all fall and winter. He may be a thousand years old, but he just keeps on going something wonderful.

Miss Nettie says he's too mean to die, but Miss Hagar says Miss Nettie, being Oysterback's most pre-eminent widow, is just mad that Ferrus never paid her no nevermind down the road. Some of the folks that live up Back Creek way, the ones that roll and shake in church, say that Ferrus is a witch because he's got a peculiar talent; he predicts things.

Now Ferrus, being a man and being human, every once in a great while calls up those half-mad black labs of his and piles into his old, old pickup truck and comes down to the Blue Crab Tavern where the boys, and some of the girls, too, all hang out of a night.

He never makes no great nevermind but always sits down to the south end of the bar by the ice machine and drinks a depth bomb or six. He says he got in the habit in the Great War, but what a depth bomb is is something even Junie Redmond won't drink; it's a mug of Heaven Hill with a shot glass of Bud dropped into it. And don't you think Ferrus pays for his own drinks, either; the boys, they do pick up his tab, having learned respect for their elders, unlike these foreigners who come in here from the Western Shore, Miss Nettie says.

Now, Miss Hagar Jump, she says Ferrus don't take any magazines, nor even a newspaper, and he doesn't have a TV, or even a radio. He does get the Sears catalog, but I don't see how that connects with his predicting. See, the thing of it is, setting out eel pots is thirsty work, and right after Ferrus sets out his eel pots, he comes down to the Blue Crab and predicts the Academy Awards. Hasn't missed once in the sixteen-odd years since I turned twenty-one and got to go to drink in the Blue Crab, either.

Late Saturday night, he came in and sat down, and even the boys stopped playing pool. Desiree Grinch, the bartender, set out his depth bomb right away, and Ferrus just chugged it down the way he always does. Desiree made him another, and Ferrus started in.

"Best Actress!" he shouted, looking around the room through those old rheumy eyes of his, half buried in wrinkles, his old Patamoke Seafood cap pulled down over his big, bushy eyebrows, just challenging us all to say him no. "Jessica Tandy's a shoo-in. She's got a track record, she deserves it. Everyone up against her's a bimbo anyway. Fine looker, that Jessica Tandy."

Nobody said anything. They just all gathered around, the way we do every year. I was kind of glad Hume Cronyn didn't hear Ferrus though; might have made him mad, since he is married to Miss Tandy.

"Best Actor! Morgan Freeman!" Ferrus said after a healthy swallow off his depth bomb. "He's good, and the Academy's feelin' guilty about overlooking Spike Lee! Kenny Branagh's a Brit—and he ain't no Olivier. Olivier wuz Olivier, that's that!"

The room sighed. A ball fell into the well in the pool table.

He drained his drink; Desiree built another. I never saw her move that big behind in those orange stretch pants that fast in my life. "Best Supporting Actor! A tough call! Probably either a split between Aykroyd and Washington, but my money's on Washington! Hollywood likes historical movies!"

Desiree put his drink in front of him. The juke all of a sudden kicked in, the way those stupid computerized things do, and someone pulled the plug. We were rapt.

Ferrus was hunkered down inside of his old field coat. His wrists stuck out of those frayed sleeves as thin and brittle as old driftwood. He looked all around himself, and he looked fierce.

"Best Picture," he said hoarsely. He looked like one of those prints of the meaner Old Testament prophets that used to hang in the Sunday school room. The cranky ones like Jeremiah and Ezekiel who were always warning everyone to clean up their acts or else. Oh, Ferrus was fierce now; he was working his way up to his grand finale, and it was Nelly bar the door. He took a big swallow off his depth bomb and looked slowly around at us all. "Best Picture," Ferrus repeated. "*Field of Dreams!*"

There was a sound in the room, the sound like the wind makes when it moves through a stand of pine trees at the edge of a soybean field.

"No," somebody said, in half a whisper, as if they wouldn't believe what Ferrus had just said.

"*Field of Dreams,*" Ferrus repeated. "Everybody loves a baseball picture." He looked as old and mean as a snapping turtle up a cove as he drained his drink, called up his dogs, and went out into the night again.

Well, I don't know. Everybody's got to be wrong sometime. I just loved *Miss Daisy,* cried and cried at the end. Huddie liked *Field of Dreams,* but then he's a pitcher for the Blue Crab Jimmies, our softball team.

Junie Redmond as usual is not impressed. He wants to know why Ferrus can't predict something useful, like the lottery or the Super Bowl. Junie don't like movies much since those Hollywood film people came to Oysterback that time. But that's another story entirely.

Over to Omar Hinton's Store

O mar Hinton's store sits at the corner of Log Cabin Point Road and
Razor Strap Lane, just far enough from where you live that you
can't just stroll over and buy a quart of two-percent milk and a can of
Happy Cat, but not so far that you don't feel guilty every time you get in
the car to drive.

Although Omar has taken to stocking a few bottles of Perrier in the
cooler, just to the left of the King Cobra Malt Liquor, he really doesn't
get that many strangers shopping there. Most of the foreigners from the
Western Shore take one look at that big old stuffed chicken hawk, poised
to swoop, that's been hanging behind the counter for the past forty years
and go right out again.

On any blowing day, you will find the usual collection of retired
watermen and farmers gathered around the pot-bellied stove having an
Oysterback breakfast, a bottle of R.C. Cola and a Little Debbie Snack
Cake, and doing what old men do best when they get away from the
women: talk about the past and tell bigger and better lies than their
neighbors. And what they love best is a new audience.

There was one day last fall when the wind was out of the northeast
and the rain was battering against the store windows. All the old gentle-
men were gathered on their benches, getting a little bored, when the
strange man walked in.

Well, they all knew he was up to no good, because he was wearing a
suit and carrying a briefcase, and even Omar had to raise his eyebrows
up to where his hairline used to be when the man asked for someone
named Wilbur Rivers, talking real slow, as if he thought none of them
could speak English.

It was so quiet you could hear Captain Hardee Swann shifting his
upper plate, which he does when he's thinking hard. "Wilbur Rivers?"
he said slowly, tugging at his ear. "I knew a Wilbur Rivers, back in '59,
'60. Lived over to Uranusville. Married a Bugg."

"Married Inez Bugg. Or was it Juanita?" Bosley Grinch asked, without opening his eyes. "Their mother played the piano over at the Jewel

Theatre when they had silent movies. Named her daughters after Rudolph Valentino's girlfriends in the movies."

"Naw, that was Bunky Bugg. Lived out on Old Route 50. Raised minks. Smelly little creatures, minks. Now, he married a Tump. Not one of the Jesterville Tumps, but one of the Tumps from over to Eldorado. Her mother was a Whortley."

"Any relation to the Whortleys up the road?" asked Faraday Hicks, known throughout the Delmarva region as the tuba-playing soybean farmer. He was peeling his nails with a Barlow knife, tossing the peelings into the stove.

"No, but they were related to the Winters that lived down the road," Hardee said thoughtfully. "Elzee Winters was a first cousin to Ray Whortley. Or was it Hurley Whortley?"

"Naw, Hurley Whortley was a foreigner from Cambridge. Now *he* married twice. Once to Elsie Shays, and once to poor Mina Harker, the one who went crazy after the war and tried to flush the laundry down the toilet. There was always bad blood in the Harkers."

"Buck Harker," Omar Hinton said from behind the counter where he was pricing a case of Indian Quarter Locally Grown Red Ripe Tomatoes.

"Clifton T. Perkins is where they sent *him*. Burned that workboat to the waterline," Bosley said matter-of-factly.

"Burned down the house."

There was a moment's silence, in which Omar put a dollar in the register and bought himself an instant Lotto ticket. While he was scraping the silver stuff off with the coin from the Need a Penny Take a Penny Have a Penny Give a Penny bowl, Captain Hardee Swann cleared his throat.

"His brother used to roller skate to church every Sunday. And him a grown man," Faraday Hicks murmured, but the stranger had fled, leaving the bells on the door jingling.

"Didn't mean to."

A companionable silence descended on the little company, and the only sound was the digestive flatulence of Omar's black Lab Warner, who had spread himself out on a carpet sample before the stove, dreaming the dreams of an old dog.

No one even looked up when Wilbur Rivers returned from a trip to the Port-O-San in the back yard. He took a bag of peanuts off the rack, opening it with his teeth.

As he poured the peanuts into his R.C. Cola, he looked around. "Did I miss anything?" he asked.

Tales from the Classifieds:
More Stuff from the *Bugeye*

Deadline for classifieds is Thursday at noon the week before publication unless Poot has an appointment with his chiropractor and takes the copy to the printer on Friday morning instead.—ED.

• • •

LOST: In the vicinity of Black Dog Road and Razor Strap Landing: pearl and gold plate ankle bracelet as seen on HSN on Saturday night after the Elks Dance. May have fallen out of black Trans-Am. Name plate says Tawnee. Reward. Call 555-1919. If a man answers hang up and try later.

• • •

LOST: Miniature poodle, male, dyed Hubba Hubba Pink, wearing cute little hot pink and white angora fluffy sweater, matching tam and painted toenails. Rhinestone collar, name tag: "Preciousness." Last seen vic. Dr. Miller Drive during Wed. afternoon DAR Canasta Club. Very delicate, unused to outdoors, needs special diet doggie food, can't sleep w/o special cushion. Owner distraught. Reward. Call 555-9486.

• • •

LOST: Will the person who took my size 16 dove gray ladies' wool coat with the mother-of-pearl buttons off the coat rack down to the Fellowship Hall last Saturday night at the Tater Tot Casserole Covered Dish Casino Night and left a size 10 charcoal gray wool coat not one half as nice please return my coat to the church coat rack? If you do, I will not tell anyone what I found in your pockets. Call Mrs. Reverend Briscoe, Parsonage, Oysterback Hardshell Methodist Church.

• • •

LOST: Large ms. "Socio-historical Overview of Oysterback MD" in brown paper bag over to the harbor. Only copy, LARGE reward. See Prof. Shepherd, Blue Crab Tavern, any evening.

• • •

PERSONAL: Earlene, please come home. The State's Attorney says she won't prosecute if you apologize to Wanda and Mookie and buy a new bug zapper. Carl repainted the Zamboni. All is forgiven. I wuv you Tootsieburger. Delmar P.

PERSONAL: Ready to Commit: SWM, 30, ISO S/D/F 25–45. If you like long walks in the rain, the ocean, blazing fireplaces, romantic music, old movies, the Orioles, country living, Trivial Pursuit, nice restaurants, and small engine repair, maybe we were made for each other. Reply w/ photo small engine, Box 20, the *Bugeye*.

• • •

NOTICE: I, Ferrus T. Buckett will not be responsible for any debts incurred by me when I am sleepwalking, especially the turkey and mayo subs over to Omar Hinton's and the cheese crackers from Ray Bob's Gas 'n' Go over to Wallopsville unless I sign for them first. I am serious about this.

• • •

NOTICE: The Tuesday Nite Bowling League will meet Thursdays until further notice or the backhoe is recovered. Imogene Redmond, Pres.

• • •

NOTICE: FENG SHUI AEROBICS CLASS: Learn Chinese interior design while you exercise away that holiday flab. Starts Monday night at the Community Center. See Hagar Jump over to the P.O. for details.

• • •

THANK YOU ST. JUDE FOR PUTTING THE WART CURSE ON MY NEXT DOOR NEIGHBOR WHO BOUGHT HIS PUNK KID AN A.T.V.— H.H.P.

• • •

WILL TRADE: 25 stuffers, slightly mildewed, for information leading to identification and slow torture of person or persons responsible for my citation by the Goose Nazis Jan 21 for hunting over bait. Reply to S. Meachum, Inmate 5745-3924, Devanaux County Detention Center, Smallsberry.

• • •

WILL TRADE: Two tickets to ProFish Bass-O-Rama Convention in Ocean City for secret to reaching Level 6 in Super Mario Chamber of Doom. Call Hudson Swann, after 3.

• • •

SALE/TRADE: Wash and Wear Designer Label Second Wedding Dress, ivory, size 10, best offer or Elvis Wedgwood Commemorative dinner set for 8. See Desiree, Blue Crab Tavern during business hours. NO PHONE CALLS PLEASE. THIS MEANS YOU EARL DON.

• • •

FOUND: Dog, eating out of the compost and rolling in the manure pile, small, very macho, breed unknown, poss. poodle with bad haircut, habits. No collar, tags lost but responds to "Butch" and loves to go gunning, swimming, out w/kids, eat dead crabs. May have rolled in pink paint. Owner may claim by identifying and paying damages, vet bills for my Labrador. See Doreen Redmond, Curl Up 'n' Dye Salon de Beaute, Oysterback.

Huddie Ponders the Ultimate Question

N ow, you take men: just when you think you've got them all figured out, one of them will come along and knock you for a loop. And I, Desiree Grinch, proprietor of the Blue Crab Tavern, know a thing or two about the gender, having been married at various times to four of them.

It so happens the other afternoon that it was business as normal down to the Blue Crab. Beth was in the kitchen, little Olivier was under the pool table teething on my porcelain Elvis Commemorative Bell, and Professor Shepherd, who lost his tenure over to the college and has to live on his boat out back, was at the bar making notes for the book he says he's going to write about us all. And then Hudson Swann comes in.

Well, I sensed something was wrong right away; he had that I've-just-been-snuck-up-from-behind-and-kicked-hard look that men tend to get when they've been confronted with some thought they don't under-stand. And when he took his usual seat up to the bar and lit a Camel, I didn't say anything. I just drew him a beer and slid it across the counter at him. Hudson just sat there and looked at it for a good long moment, so I went on about my business, getting up on the ice chest and chalking "Oysters Desiree $5.95" up on the blackboard, for the dinner crowd.

You see, usually you have to give Huddie Swann a minute or two to collect his thoughts. I'm not going to say he's inarticulate, but he can spend a right good amount of time stumbling around in the dark looking for the right words.

Finally, he clears his throat, pushes his hat up with the ball of his thumb, takes a swallow off his beer, and says, "Listen here, Des, do you ever think about God?"

Well, I almost fell over and took the chalkboard with me, I was that surprised. I had to think that over for a moment, since Hudson is the least churchy man I know.

"Well, of course I think about God," I replied at last. "In fact, when I finally meet Her, there are questions I would like to ask."

I guess that was the answer he wanted, because he looked a little relieved. At least he nodded and spread his hands out flat on the counter and worked his lips a little while before anything come out.

"You know, when you're out there on the water, on *Miss Jeanne,* and you've got the engine running and the patent tong motor running, and it's up and down, up and down, the tong pullin' a lick, pullin' a lick, and you're cullin' for all you're worth, trying to catch your limit before three o'clock, there's not much you can do, you know, with your mind except *think.*"

He looked at me so pathetic I didn't have the heart to say well, that must be a new experience for you, which sounds good but really isn't true anyway, so I just nodded.

It took a minute, but he continued on. "You know, you're just out there in all weather, and you're cold and you're wet and you think about stuff like what you did twenty years ago, and should you have done it different, or about your kids, or the Bay, or this thought, which just come all over me at once."

Then he leans over, so close I can see how black his pupils are and how green his eyes, as green as the Bay, and asks me, very seriously, "When you're on God's culling board, are you box or are you cull?"

Well, even I, Desiree Grinch, did not have the answer to that one.

I guess it was a good thing that Professor Shepherd leans over at that moment and slaps Huddie on the back. "Why, you're cull!" he exclaims. "You're always cull, Huddie!"

Hudson looked real relieved. I guess that was the answer he wanted, because he bought the professor a drink and invited him to play some pool.

I was still sitting there with my mouth open when Beth Redmond stuck her head out of the kitchen. She looks at those two then looks at me and shakes her head.

"I'd rather be spat," she says, and winks at me so hard I just had to laugh.

The Wisdom of Miss Nettie's Fritters

On the kitchen wall, the cat clock ticks away the twilight hours. The rhinestone eyes slide one way, the black plastic tail the other.

Miss Nettie Leery stubs out her Salem in the big glass ashtray on the table. When her visitor is not looking, she glances first up at the cat clock, then out the window, where the snow is falling in small, mean flakes. Deep inside the still, darkened parlor, the wind moans and whines in the chinks beneath the doors, feeling at the window sashes, looking for entry. But the kitchen is warm and steamy.

"Listen to that. She's up and down the mast tonight," Miss Nettie says, rising from the table and brushing cigarette ash from her massive bosom. "Don't think your folks will come lookin' for you on a night like this, no matter what you did. Anyway, they canceled the Rutger Hauer Film Festival up to the Community Center. So, as long as you're here wyn't you stay and see how I make my oyster fritters? It's a family secret, passed from my grandmother to me, and from me to you."

Miss Nettie opened the refrigerator, taking things out and setting them on the counter. "They're not gourmet or fancy, just plain Oyster-back cooking," she tells her visitor, grunting as she bends to retrieve the big iron skillet from the place where it lives in the oven. "Fetch me over that big ironstone bowl, that's a lamb," she says, dolloping out two walnut-sized spoonfuls of Crisco into the pan. "Now, you set that on low heat while you build your batter.

"That young doctor would have a fit if he could see me makin' oyster fritters. When I was your age, we fried 'em in lard. Four times a year, Dad would go up to Baltimore on the skipjack and come back with a barrel of flour, a sack of sugar, and a fifty-pound can of lard. He didn't know nothing about cholesterol, and he lived to be ninety-seven!

"No one on our side of the family's ever had a heart attack. Cholesterol! Huh!" She breaks an egg on the side of the bowl, whisking it with a fork. Opening a pint mason jar of shucked oysters, she spoons them into the bowl and stirs them carefully.

"I was just your age when my Me-Mom showed me how to make

oyster fritters. That gold and red set of china was her wedding set. It come all the way from China on a clipper ship. Keep an eye on that skillet, don't let it heat up too fast. No, I daresay that your mom and daddy won't come lookin' for you on a night like this, no matter what you broke," she assures her visitor.

She opens the red and white rooster canister on the counter and dumps about a quarter cup of flour into the bowl with the oysters. Then she adds salt and pepper. "Get out in the pantry and fetch me the baking powder. Not the baking soda, the baking powder. Now, watch. You add a teaspoon to the batter, then three tablespoons Half and Half.

"When I was your age, I knocked over my mother's Chelsea Bow cat, smashed it into a thousand pieces. Oh, she was fit to be tied! I went to *my* Me-Mom and hid there. Now, watch me: I fold it all together, I don't stir it up with this here wooden spoon. You stir, you break the oysters apart. Is that Crisco smokin' in the skillet now? Fine."

Carefully, Miss Nettie ladles the batter into the skillet. "Now, some of the ladies at church, they make fritters the size of a pancake. Use pancake mix, too. Don't let me catch you doin' that! You want your fritters to be the size of the mouth of a drinking glass, no bigger." As the batter hits the hot pan, it sizzles, sending a delicious aroma into the moist and steamy kitchen.

"Now, when the edges of the fritters are crisp and brown, and the batter's bubbling on the inside, it's time to turn it. You run and get a jar of those green beans I canned last August and put that in the microwave. And get the silver out and set the table. We'll use the gold and red china tonight, for special. And we'll have some of that watermelon pickle and a taste of that chow-chow you like, OK?"

The fritters slowly turn from buff to crisp golden brown, and Miss Nettie flips them over the spatula. "Now," she says, "Run and get me a grocery sack from the shelf. A paper one, not one of those nasty plastic ones. That's what we drain the fritters on."

From somewhere, the cat appears, attracted by the smell of food. It rubs against Miss Nettie's legs. "Beggar," she says, but she slips it a small oyster anyway. The cat seizes it and disappears.

As Miss Nettie eases the fritters from the skillet on to the coarse brown paper bag, the wind picks up, howling and rattling at the kitchen windows. "That's the devil trying to escape the weather," Miss Nettie says complacently.

The fritters, round and crispy, stain the coarse paper dark brown. Miss Nettie ladles out more batter into the skillet. "Never stop when the pan's hot," she says.

Beneath the whining of the blizzard, she hears a sound and she cocks her head to one side, listening. A faint smile plays on her lips.

"Best to set another place," she commands. "We're going to have some more company. Yes, I imagine it is your Daddy, but I doubt that he'll be angry with you by now. Don't you think that he's had time to realize that you're more important to him than a fishing reel? By the time he's realized you're gone, and he's driven all over the place looking for you, he'll be more scared than angry. And hungry, too. Oyster fritters are a great pacifier for anyone."

Miss Nettie watches, unsurprised, as the headlights of a truck move slowly up her lane. "How did I know it was him? How did I know it was him? Why child, I'd know the sound of that truck anywhere! Heard it all the way down at the corner of Black Dog Road. You go put the porch light on for him, and tell your Daddy not to come any further than the mud room in his boots. I don't want my clean floors tracked up with mud. Run, now, don't let him stumble around in that snow!"

When she is alone in the kitchen, she helps herself to a small, beautifully round fritter. The cake is crumbly and light; the warm oysters break apart in her mouth, delicate and salty. Miss Nettie closes her eyes. "Perfect," she sighs. "Just perfect."

After the Funeral of Haney Sparks

R everend Alfred Briscoe cast an experienced eye over the bounty of funeral meats on the table and, with a sigh, helped himself to just a tad of stuffed ham, candied yams, a crabcake, some stringbean and mushroom casserole, watermelon pickle, chow-chow, and both a beaten biscuit and a piece of cornbread. Balancing his paper plate carefully on his arm, he wove through the buffet line and settled himself on a glider on the sunporch. He nodded companionably at Parsons Dreedle, the funeral director, as that worthy settled himself on the other end of the glider with his own brimming plate.

Mr. Dreedle was still talking to young Dr. Samuel Wheedleton, the town's new medic, as he broke his cornbread and sipped iced tea from a paper cup. "Ella could've shot him *dead* at high noon downtown, and there wouldn't have been a jury in Santimoke County who would've convicted her, Haney was that mean. If you ast me, there's a lotta people in here today who just come to the funeral to make sure Haney Sparks was dead." Parsons dug into a corn fritter with gusto. " 'Course, you an' me, we could've set 'em straight on that, hey, Doc?"

The young doctor, still new to the Eastern Shore and unused to Parsons Dreedle's plain way of speaking, gave a covert glance into the living room where the rest of the mourners, the nonprofessionals, so to speak, were balancing laden paper plates on the knees of their black dresses and dark suits. Their voices had settled into a low and happy hum as they addressed their feast. Mrs. Ella Sparks, the newly bereaved widow, was as famous for her fine cooking as her late husband had been infamous for his deeds.

If any of the mourners, including the widow, had heard Parsons's tactless remark, they gave no indication. "Don't pay them no never-mind. It's us three they like to avoid at funerals around here," Parsons advised the young physician. "The doctor, the preacher, and the under-taker all remind them they could be next, see?" He put a large piece of ham in his mouth and sighed in bliss. "I tell you, Doc, most people around here think poor Ella was relieved of a burden when ole Haney collapsed, face down, in that plate of sweet cream giblet gravy and sour cream mashed potatoes. Dead as a doornail, he was. Massive heart attack is what you said on the death certificate, if I recall."

The doctor made some noncommittal remark, while Reverend Briscoe's expression shifted between pain and amusement. Oblivious, Mr. Dreedle plunged on. "You see any children come home for the funeral? Not one. Who's to blame for that?" He forked up a generous helping of oyster pie. "Haney Sparks was as mean as a snake. Listen, if it had been my choice, I would soon as buried him at a crossroads with a stake in his heart as put him in the churchyard after all the misery he caused. And fat? My land! As it was, it took me and both my boys to lift him on the draining table and the trocar—"

"There is a limit to Christian forbearance," Reverend Briscoe broke in. "Why Ella took him back after that last disgraceful episode, I do not know." He looked as if he would have liked to say more, but he contented himself with addressing his plate. "As her minister, I advised against it."

"Ella's a saint. She took him back, in spite of it all," Mr. Dreedle growled. He was known to have been sweet on the former Ella Sweeny in high school. "And from the time he come back, he never shifted his worthless carcass any further than from the TV to the bed to the kitchen table. Bad back, he says. Bad back, ha! She waited on him hand and foot. The only exercise he ever took was when he put himself in the truck and went to the Blue Crab Tavern for a cheesesteak and a quart of vodka, every afternoon. Made poor Ella walk everywhere! Saw her one morning walking all the way down to Omar Hinton's store after cream. Cream! Milk in his coffee wouldn't do! Ate his breakfast up in the bed. She served him on a tray. Every morning, the same thing. Fried him up six eggs and a half pound of bacon, three, four cat's-head biscuits with butter. Then, for lunch, he'd eat dried beef gravy and half a pecan pie, then that cheesesteak and fries for a snack, and a big ole slab a prime rib and gravy for dinner. Laid up in front of the TV smoking them cigars and drinkin' that vodka all afternoon and night, while poor Ella slaved over a hot stove. As thin as a bird she is, too, from working herself to the bone!" Indignantly, the undertaker bit into a snowflake roll. He looked from the doctor to the preacher. "It passeth understanding, just like it says in the Bible." He was proud of his knowledge of Scripture and the poetry of Robert Service.

"Ella must have loved Haney right to death," Reverend Briscoe sighed. He was still awed by the strange twists of human nature.

The sound of Dr. Wheedleton's laugh startled both men; the young doctor was a very serious person. "Loved him to death," he repeated. "Yes, I suppose you could say that she loved him to death." He looked from the undertaker to the minister, a faint sardonic smile flickering behind his glasses. "When Mr. Sparks returned to town, Mrs. Sparks insisted he see me about his back." The doctor took a deep breath and lowered his voice. "There was nothing wrong with his back" he said. "But his arteries—they were so clogged with cholesterol you couldn't have pushed a microbe through them with a stick of dynamite. And his heart . . ." he shook his head. "I told Mrs. Sparks if she wanted her husband to live, she should put him on a whole new regimen. Exercise, no smoking, no fats, no sugar, no cholesterol. *If she wanted him to live.*" Dr. Wheedleton peered at his companions over his thick glasses. "It was my professional opinion that Mr. Sparks was a thoroughly unpleasant human being," he added.

Reverend Briscoe opened and closed his mouth, but Mr. Dreedle, whose wits were quicker, laughed. "Haney Sparks always did used to say that Ella's cooking was to die for!" he exclaimed.

The Prince of Tilghman Island

Although there is not a dogwood to be seen in Dogwood Cove, there are a couple of dogs lying in the shade of the pickup trucks, watching with bored canine interest as Captain Randolph Murphy patiently explains why the skipjacks aren't coming in under sail. "This time of year, they just don't have the crew to put up the sails," he is telling a Baltimore couple. "So they come in under power."

They look like they are from a Norman Rockwell painting titled "Tourists." Pa is laden with camera equipment, snapping picture after picture of the waterman. Ma is wearing ankle socks and health sandals. She adjusts her cat's-eye glasses and fans her Mamie Eisenhower bangs with a hand. The late afternoon sun is warm.

"Did you hear that, Mother?" the man asks. "There's not enough wind." One more picture of Randolph is exposed. Randolph smiles patiently beneath his Bay Hundred Ducks Unlimited hat.

Mother squints as the sticks of the dredge boats heave into view. "They're not pretty like sailboats, are they?" she asks dubiously, looking at the rusty hulls and the worn docks.

"They're beautiful," Randolph says. "Last working sail on the Bay." Behind his sunglasses, he frowns just a little. His tone is almost gentle. It is said if Randolph were left in the middle of Bangkok in his underwear in the morning, by sundown he would have a new wardrobe, fifty best friends, and the best poker game in town.

"They call him the Prince of Tilghman Island, Mother," the man says. "Are you writing all this down?"

The Norman Rockwells are part of a slide club. They are doing Maryland in day trips, going from place to place taking pictures of the sights. "We only have about a thousand slides, so we really have to get going," Mother says to the reporter, who has perched on the tailgate of the Prince of Tilghman Island's macho Ford pickup. "The big slide meet is in June."

Good luck or simple faith in the goodness of man has brought these people to the island, where, as these things work out, the Norman Rockwells have made contact, without even half trying, with the man the reporter has been searching high and low after for well over half a year.

True to his princely nature, the Prince of Tilghman Island, Captain Randolph Murphy, has turned up far from where he said he would be and without any memory of having made a rendezvous. Fortunately, the reporter knows his haunts, and only had to look in two or three of them before spotting the famous copper-colored truck with the D.U. stickers. Men, especially Tilghman men, are never where they say they're going to be, but usually where they feel like being. Like God, they are never on time, but they are always there when you need them. Or almost always. Tilghman's not so big that you can't find someone if you look hard enough.

Since he sold the bar, the Prince has spent several months in seclusion. Now he is fooling his detractors by coming back better than ever. "I'm tanned, rested, and ready," he says. Twenty-five pounds lighter and back on the water, he is grinning like a Cheshire cat.

"The Prince of Tilghman Island." Mother Rockwell has to write that down in her little notebook. The reporter imagines that it's going to make interesting talk back at the slide meet. The Norman Rockwells are so cute, and so tiny beside the six-foot-something Prince, that you just want to take them home and put them up on the shelf next to your fish decoys.

Mother Rockwell is clearly disappointed. She wants things to be quaint and charming rather than gritty and dirty as they are here in Dogwood Cove. She and Father take off in search of soft-shell crabs.

Now Captain Norman Murphy and Andy Miller have come to lean into the Prince's pickup truck. They have brought ice-cold beverages, and the Murphy cousins and Mr. Miller lean into the pickup as if expecting a high wind to sweep off the Bay and blow them all away. Perhaps after a lifetime spent on pitching decks, it seems natural to cling to something for support. Pickup truck groups are a common sight here in the cove, but maybe these men see more than the mysterious bits of marine engine and bushel baskets in the bed. They stare down into the truck with great interest.

Since the reporter is ostensibly here to check on crab conditions, Norman Murphy shrugs. He has a blue and red tattoo on one bicep that says "Heather." "Maybe three bushels," he says. "Them crabs ain't gonna smell that eel and come crawling across the river after it. You gotta go get 'em."

"I been bringin' 'em up with the mud still on 'em," Randolph says.

"When the weather warms up, they'll come in," Andy Miller opines.

Norman Murphy turns the talk toward Bay ecology. "Red tide," he says. "Used to be that you never saw it over here, even when the wind blew hard." He blames it on Glidden Paint and Proctor and Gamble spilling chemicals into the Bay.

"Red tide," Norman Murphy repeats.

"Micro-organic blossoms," Randolph says, savoring the feel of the words on his tongue.

"I was over to Cockey's in Claiborne, once, in the middle of one of those red tides, and I heard this scratch, scratch, scratch. I thought it was maybe rats trapped in my hull, and I looked overboard. It was crabs, scuttling up the railway, out of the water. There was no oxygen in the water at all. They were coming onto land in search of oxygen because they were drowning in the water."

Norman Murphy frowns, looks over his shoulder across the harbor. "Here comes your wife, Andy," he remarks.

A woman pushing a stroller is approaching us. She seems very young, but so does her husband.

"That's your wife and my baby," Randolph laughs.

Unfazed, Andy shakes his head.

But when eight-month-old Callie and her mother come up to the truck, Randolph sweeps her out of her stroller. "What have we here?" he asks her, and Callie gurgles happily.

There is something endearing about the way in which the big burly waterman holds the small baby. The Prince of Tilghman Island, secure enough in his masculinity to cuddle an infant right in front of his peers, the reporter thinks, but would never say aloud.

"You need one of those, Randy," someone says.

The prince just grunts.

Callie laughs delightedly. The Prince of Tilghman Island is hell on women of all ages.

Latest News from the *Oysterback Bugeye*

LISA ANNE HACKETT expects to be released from jail in time to ride on the Oysterback Volunteer Fire Department Float in the Fireman's Parade in Ocean City. When asked if the conviction would affect her title as Miss Oysterback, Lisa's mother, Mrs. Carlotta Hackett, said she doubted it, since she had the only pink Cadillac convertible in town and she was not about to allow runner-up Rikki Jane Insley to put that tacky peach prom gown on *her* upholstery.

• • •

A MILDEW PATCH in the shape of ELVIS PRESLEY has miraculously appeared in the mud room of Miss Nettie Leery's home. Elvis fan Desiree Grinch has erected an altar before the spot, in which the King appears to be nearing the end of his career. . . . Visitors have congregated on Miss Nettie's lawn for several days in hopes of a glimpse of the Elvis apparition.

• • •

OMAR HINTON has added a full-service fax machine to his line of state-of-the-art communications at Hinton's Store. In a brief ceremony, postmaster Hagar Jump christened the machine by faxing an indignant letter to Congressman Orville Orvall about the potholes on Jesterville Road.

• • •

CITIZENS OF OYSTERBACK were all thrilled to see Junie Redmond and Huddie Swann preserving our God-given right to burn fossil fuels on last week's edition of "America's Funniest Home Videos." . . . No damage was done to Sheik Abdul Ben Hassein, the seafood plant, or the Blue Crab Jimmies' Softball Trophy, although Desiree Grinch has announced that the Sheik and Huddie are banned from the Blue Crab for a week.

• • •

JOHNNY RAY INSLEY's campaign for Third District was derailed last night in a mudslinging debate at the Community Center between Deputy Insley and the League of Women Voters, who denounced Insley as a "bozo."

• • •

BOOT WILLIS reports that he has brought up a crab the size of a size-13 Redball boot. Those who wish to view the giant crab may do so by stopping by the Blue Crab Tavern, where Desiree is planning to make the world's largest crabcake.

• • •

OYSTERBACK SENIOR CENTER is sponsoring a bus trip to Washington next Thursday. In the morning, the group will view "Treasures of the Gods" at the Smithsonian. In the afternoon, they will see a performance of "Much Ado About Nothing" at the Folger, and that evening, they will attend a Whitesnake concert at RFK. Tickets may be purchased at Omar Hinton's store.

• • •

SHAMPOO GIRL FERN LEGUME was honored with a Tupperware Bridal Shower by her fellow employees and clients at Doreen's Curl Up 'n' Dye Salon de Beaute. Fern received many fine storage containers and a colander.

• • •

MR. AND MRS. ELMO SKINNER are in town visiting their cousins, Capt. and Mrs. Lennie Skinner. Mrs. Elmo Skinner is the 1983 winner of the Slim Jims Bake-Off Contest with her recipe for Slim Jim Lasagna.

• • •

HELGA WALLOP, editor of this paper, will offer a Crash Craft Course at the Community Center for anyone interested in making a caddy for their *TV Guide*. Bring a roll of scotch tape, a package of onion rings, and a crescent wrench.

• • •

HOUSEHOLDERS ARE WARNED that bluefish season is here. Check your doorsteps in the morning for surprise offerings from fisherman friends.

• • •

THE OYSTERBACK MOSQUITO FESTIVAL will be held Saturday. The Loyal Order of Squirrels, Lodge No. 164, held their annual Poker Tournament and Fisherman's Liar Contest at the Fire Hall. Special guests included the police.

• • •

THE BLUE CRAB TAVERN JIMMIES pitched a shutout game against the Wingo, Virginia, Lounge Lizards, ending the seasons in second place. . . . Lizards shortstop Snake Wingate challenged Jimmies batter Paisley Redmond to an arm-wrestling match to settle the dispute about the tar ball.

THE FIRST ANNUAL MEETING of the Oysterback Gunning Widows Club will be held on Saturday at the new Mall. Bring your credit cards!

• • •

A DECISION handed down by Circuit Court Judge William S. Horne awarded the Winnebago, the antique beer-can collection, and the auto-graphed 8 × 10 glossy of Rutger Hauer to Winona. George received the microwave, the subscription to *Soldier of Fortune,* and visitation rights to the metal detector. . . . The couple agreed to share the season tickets to the Metropolitan Opera Series, as well as custody of the sea monkeys.

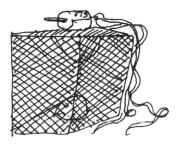

Half a Boy and Half a Man

There's nothing lonelier than a deserted bar on a Monday night when it's just you and the TV. Have you noticed that "Designing Women" isn't funny since Charlene and Suzanne left? I have. Maybe that's why I am sitting here, looking out the window, watching Michael Ruarke play air ball.

Watching that kid standing out there in the darkness all alone, I know he isn't just hanging out on the Blue Crab softball field, pretending to pitch. There's probably not a fan alive who hasn't played air ball; in your imagination, you're out there in the stadium, it's the top of the ninth, you've walked one and struck two out, the fans are going wild, the team is counting on you, and you're a legend in your own mind. When you're eighteen, that magic still works, even for a kid like Michael. Especially for a kid like Michael.

I have a strict rule for myself: Never feed the strays. I, Desiree Grinch, proprietor of the Blue Crab Tavern, have problems getting attached to living things that die or leave. Nonetheless, I go in the kitchen and cut two big slices of my black walnut chess pie and put them on a paper plate. Well, it would just go to waste, wouldn't it? I also have a problem following my own rules.

I guess if I was anyone else, Michael would stop in mid-pitch and pretend he is doing something else. But when he sees me coming across the field, he sort of grins his lopsided grin, really putting his whole body into slamming that air ball over the plate. I could almost see it arching in a neat curve over the plate, hear the bat swish through empty air.

"Hey, Desiree," he says, hitching his West Hundred High School Baseball jacket up around his shoulders, stuffing his mitt inside for safekeeping. "Way cool, pie!" He takes the paper plate from me and just launches into that food.

When you're eighteen, 6-foot-2, and weigh 195, I guess you're always hungry. Maybe it's the moving; kids are always bopping, as if there's some kind of internal music that only they can hear, some rhythm that forces them to sway and jitter all the time. Sometimes I hear that music myself, on a spring night with a full moon and the town just a string of lights along the river, summer spreading out in front of me like a promise.

"Your mom got company over to the house again?" I ask. I could say more, a whole lot more, but I don't.

Me, I think people should have to have a license to have kids.

"Yeah," Michael says around bites. For him, it's business as usual; when he sees the boyfriend's truck going down the road, he knows he can go home. "This is real good pie, Desiree."

"I guess you think so, the way you inhaled it. Did you get your homework done?"

"Did it in study hall. You should've seen me at practice today, Desiree. Coach says he's got a friend who's a scout for the college. Wants me to talk to him about a scholarship."

He folds up the paper plate and pushes it into his pocket, then does a sort of turn, those big stupid sneakers they all wear dragging in the dust. Finally he grins at me, that lopsided grin, and I know he's really excited and trying to hide it, like maybe something this great will be taken away from him. It wouldn't be the first time.

"Michael, that's great! See, I told you, you could do it, if you just keep that pitch smooth, from the shoulder. I am so proud of you, kid." And dammit, I am. Still half a boy and half a man, Michael's turned out as a decent human being; he's never taken on that hard, mean edge some kids like him have.

"Desiree, it came to me that I could have anything, even those stars up there, if I wanted 'em bad enough." He pitched to the sky. If he'd had a ball, it would have gone to the moon right then.

"Yes, you can," I say. "You can have anything you want, if you're willing to work for it." Then I have to laugh, to hear myself handing out advice on how to lead a life. "I guess I sound like someone's mother," I mumble.

"You don't seem anything like a mother to *me,*" Michael says, and puts his arm around my shoulders so that I have to look up at him, reading his face, so serious it could break your heart.

Never feed the strays.

Floater

Deputy Johnny Ray Insley speaks:
When he didn't come in by seven o'clock, his girlfriend called us. She was scared; we could hear the kids crying in the background. Chief Briscoe called the fire company and the Coast Guard; the DNR boys, they come on in off their radio when one of the boys from Oysterback called in he'd found Devlin Dean's boat adrift off Log Cabin Point. There was no sign of Devy, just everything the way you'd have it patent tonging, and his boat was out of gas. That was a bad sign right there. We looked all night and didn't find him.

Next morning, Chief put them big old grappling hooks aboard his boat and a couple lengths of line, and I knew, by the look on his face, that he'd done this before. You could tell he didn't like it none. I was new then, and didn't know that much about the water. My people were all Wallopsville farmers, so I was used to a different set of troubles.

Don't you see, it can happen to anyone out there. All you need is a high wind, some big swells, a careless move. You just don't know what, all the things that can happen. Hell, some of these older men, they don't even know how to swim, as crazy as that sounds.

It was the day that big storm blew through the Carolinas; all we got up here was high wind and big waves. When you're young, you think you're going to live forever. You take risks. You do things on impulse, like climb up on the washboards after something that needs straightening out. They were saving to buy a house, you see. He didn't want to pay the culler's shares. If he'd had a culler, maybe he would have been all right, another man could have fished him out. You see them great big ole tongheads, the size and the weight, swinging on a big swell, and you could see how they could knock you overboard if you looked away for one second. You have to watch everything all the time. Since then, I been out a couple of times, and I seen for myself what it's like for a waterman. Overboard, them rubber boots can fill up with water and drag you right down; that time of year, hypothermia can hit you before you work them big ole boots off and get up to the surface.

When Chief threw the grappling hooks over the side, the splash they made was so loud; there was lots of boats out, but they was all going real slow, dragging the bottom. Over to that place on the Bay they call the Stones, you could feel them hooks dragging, and the boat just sort of jerked and hauled. Back and forth we went, not saying much. There wasn't much to say.

I heard someone on another boat make a joke about trolling for big bluefish. He didn't mean nothing; it was just so bad. We all do it to ease it up, make some bad joke to cut some slack. Otherwise you couldn't bear it, you see; it would break your heart, the stuff you see. No one said *drowned* or *dead,* but the thought hung in the air like a bad smell.

The sun was setting when he come up, still with one boot on him. That's why them call 'em floaters, you know. The corpse gas brings 'em up. Funny how you remember the little things, how it was flat calm, the way the sunset shone on him as he lay on the boards, the water running out of him. He'd been all chewed up by crabs, all swollen up. I watched a crab let go of Devy's finger and crawl across the deck, drop right into the bilge. It made a little splash. One boy puked over the side. The sunset was the color of blood.

Isn't it funny, the little things, the details you remember after all these years, and the big things just pass you by.

Summer Calendar, from the *Oysterback Bugeye*

A GERANIUM SALE and Microwave Cookoff Contest will be held at Oysterback Methodist Church June 3. "Cooking with Processed Cheese Food" will be the theme.

• • •

TED DI BIASE, pro wrestling's Million Dollar Man, will address the graduating class of Oysterback High School at Commencement June 7.

• • •

ANCIENT BLOOD FEUDS and high school rivalries promise to make this year's Micro Brewery League softball games the best yet! The Blue Crab Jimmies will square off against hated opponents, Wingo, Va.'s, Dew Drop Inn Lounge Lizards. Blue Crab Proprietor Desiree Grinch promises the action off the field will be even better than Junie Redmond's famous crabspit ball. Free beer, first aid, and a Blue Crab T-shirt to the first twenty-five spectators at the June 10 game under the lights in the Blue Crab's ball field.

• • •

OYSTERBACK MIDDLE SCHOOL art teacher Griselda Everdean will present her student dance troupe, Ballet Folklorico de Tilghman Island, in performance at the Community Center June 19. Ms. Everdean will solo in her acclaimed "Danse de Defiance aux Jesse Helms."

• • •

A RUMMAGE SALE AND DIALOGUE on the Historical Overviews of Sören Kierkegaard will be held June 21 at Oysterback Hardshell Methodist Church to benefit local charity Professor Shepherd, who didn't get tenure from the State College and now lives on his boat in the harbor. Miss Hagar Jump, a Little Theatre favorite, will play Kierkegaard.

• • •

THE PHYLLIS SCHAFLY CHAPTER of Submissive Wives will hold a Handiwrap lingerie show and prayer breakfast at the home of Mrs. LaMar Griswold, if LaMar isn't having his buddies over for cards that night and isn't in one of his moods, on June 3.

• • •

ONE OF THE EASTERN SHORE's most popular bands of a decade ago, Steel Trap, will be re-forming, according to keyboardist and perennial Bird Dog and the Road Kings groupie Brandi Bambi. Steel Trap, arguably the most popular band on the Shore, had almost hit the big time in a Hoffa Stadium concert in Cape May. Grits Jones, lead guitarist and singer, was arrested in mid-concert for attempting to smuggle 40 lbs. of cocaine into New Jersey in the back of his amplifier when, during a particularly heavy rendition of "Stairway to Heaven," the amplifier exploded and police rushed the stage. Out of Rahway State Prison now, Grits, Brandi, and the boys are tanned, rested, and ready to rock and roll in a tentative August date at the Hebron Hotel Party.

• • •

ONCE AGAIN, THE OYSTERBACK VFD will present a fireworks extravaganza down at the harbor on the Glorious 4th, if Hudson Swann remembers to pick up the fireworks on his way back from sneaking down to Virginia to pour sugar water into the gas tank of hated rival Lizards pitcher Snake Wingate.

• • •

THE LADIES OF OYSTERBACK METHODIST CHURCH and the Ladies' Auxiliary of the Oysterback VFD will again combine forces this year for the Oysterback Tomato Festival. Tomatoes will be the theme this year, with a tomato contest, tomato jelly, tomato pie, and new Tomato and Tater Tots Casserole recipes. The Festival will start July 17 and end July 21 with the crowning of Miss Beefsteak, the Tomato Princess. This year it has been decided that instead of sacrificing a tourist to the Tomato Fertility God, a developer will do just as well. If no developer is available, the public is reminded that Geraldo Rivera will be Master of Ceremonies this year.

• • •

AUGUST 3 HERALDS THE RETURN of the popular Spray Truck Pull and Steam Show at Widgeon Park. Bring a picnic lunch and a particle mask!

• • •

CUCUMBER NIGHT will be August 25 this year, Mrs. Nettie Leery says. Join your neighbors in leaving all those thousands of cukes that have suddenly appeared in your garden on the doorsteps of your neighbors in the dead of night! This year bluefish and excess tomatoes will also be included in the fun.

• • •

MR. EARL'S PARTY FARM will hold a Labor Day Battle of the Bands starting at dusk on Friday and continuing until the last bass player drops from exhaustion Monday afternoon. Once again, security will be provided by Satan's Psychos, Ocean City Chapter. Due to the sudden commitment of Hooley Wallop, rhythm guitarist for Steel Trap, to the Betty Ford Clinic, the band's reunion concert has been postponed indefinitely this year.

Reflections on an Oysterback Wedding

Although Hagar Jump twisted and craned her neck, it was almost impossible for her to look in the mirror and see what Doreen Redmond was doing to Hagar's hair. The mirror at Doreen's station at the Salon de Beaute was nearly covered with snaps of Doreen, her husband Junie, their three children, several generations of black Labs, and Doreen's Honorable Mention in the Mid-Atlantic Stylist's Conference Competition for Cellophaning. "Mind what you do to my bangs," Hagar said. "Last time, you left me looking like Mamie Eisenhower."

"So that's why you didn't get your hair cut before the wedding," Doreen said, shifting a wad of Nicorette from one side of her jaw to the other. "If you wouldn't take a nail scissors to 'em between cuts, they wouldn't look so bad, Hagar. Anyway, I still think that strawberries floating in champagne punch is tacky. And those matchbooks that said 'Lisa and Billy—A Perfect Match' were tacky, too." She was trying to give up three packs of Kools a day.

"Carlotta told me she saw the recipe in *Southern Living,* and it called for melon balls. Can you see melon balls floating in Carlotta's good Heisey punchbowl?"

Miss Nettie Leery, her hair half rolled into styrofoam curlers, turned to look over her shoulder at Doreen.

"Mom, if you don't hold on still, I'll never get you rolled up, and I've got an eleven o'clock," Jeanne Swann told Miss Nettie around a mouth full of hairpins. "I couldn't get past Miss Carlotta's mother-of-the-bride outfit. Desiree said Mr. Hackett took Billy Chinaberry aside about a month before the wedding and offered him all the wedding money to elope. Bill would've taken it, too, if Lisa hadn't thrown a fit and called them both cheap."

"That's men for you," Hagar Jump said darkly.

"Ain't that the truth, girl! I thought I would die of embarrassment when Junie wanted to play the spoons at the reception."

"Well, did you see poor Betty Chinaberry? Where in the world did she get that mother-of-the-groom dress? The tablecloth department at Mc-

DOREEN'S
Curl Up 'N' Dye
SALON DE BEAUTÉ

Your appointment is
Saturday, May 1st
at 9:30 am
with Doreen
wash + set/manicure

Crory's? I know Lisa's bridesmaids' dresses came from Sears, the boxes were shipped right through the post office," Hagar said.

Jeanne Swann gave a whoop. "Weren't they just awful? Apple green taffeta is what it said in the paper, but it made them all look as if they'd been *eating* green apples, if you ask me. Billy Chinaberry's sister Yvonne's too big to wear all of those big skirts and sleeves and bows; she looked just like a crocheted doll that you put on top of a toilet paper roll in that outfit. Close your eyes, Mom. I'm going to spray you now."

"I almost married Frank Chinaberry," Miss Nettie said dreamily. "He did all right with those chicken houses. He gave Billy and Lisa their own trailer to live in, right on the property."

"Me, I like a man to have a chin, thanks," Doreen said glumly. "Tell you what I think—I think Miss Carlotta picked out those bridesmaids' dresses, on purpose like, so that the other girls would look just awful. That way, when Billy seen Lisa comin' down the aisle followed by that crew, he'd *know* he made the right choice."

Doreen popped another Nicorette into her mouth. "I'm dying for a cigarette," she moaned. "It's been five hours!"

"Hang in there, gal, you can do it," Miss Nettie admonished her, wagging a finger. "Tell you what I like to die of embarrassment from was when my son-in-law started to snore in the middle of the vows."

"That was allergies, Mom!" Jeanne hissed fiercely. "And him over to her house right now, cuttin' her grass. Shame on you!"

"But he shore woke up when Lisa started to twirl those fire batons right there in the church!" Doreen laughed.

"I never heard that poor little organist, Miss Buck, play 'Close to You' so up-tempo in my life," Jeanne laughed. "She just couldn't keep up with those fire batons."

"Doesn't Desiree Grinch own a dress? I couldn't believe that outfit she wore—looked like a cowgirl, all that white leather fringe and glitter," Miss Nettie shook her head. "Don't pull my hair, Jeanne Leery! You're not too big to spank!"

"Try it, Mom," Jeanne said cheerfully, "and your hair will have such a blue rinse on it that folks will say you glow in the dark." Desiree was Jeanne's best friend. "Desiree got that outfit from the same man that made Elvis's jumpsuits."

"And did you see Lisa's silver pattern? There's so much junk on it, flowers and fruit and so forth, that the butterknife weighs about six pounds." Doreen cracked her Nicorette and shifted from foot to foot in her Nursemates. "Wait till she has to polish that stuff."

"The pattern's called Colonial Medici," Hagar said. She knew about such things.

Miss Nettie sighed. "I always cry at weddings," she said.

Snake Wingate Proposes, God Disposes

I t was the bottom of the ninth and things were not looking good for the Blue Crab Jimmies.

Snake Wingate, so named for his resemblance to a reptile, star pitcher for the Lounge Lizards, was on the mound. So far, Snake had struck out both the Redmond Brothers and Earl Don Grinch.

Desiree Grinch had been hugging second so long that her blue infield chatter was causing Lizards baseman Born Again Brumbalow to lose the razor blade he had concealed in his pocket-sized New Testament. Snake, sure he had the game tied down, was grinning his beady-eyed grin.

He had already struck Hudson out twice that day, and it looked like our boy just wasn't playing in midseason form. You could see that Snake was already anticipating striking Huddie out for the third time, just by the way he was licking the tobacco juice stain on his jaw.

In the long history of blood feuds and ancient rivalries that characterize the relationship between the towns of Oysterback and Wingo, perhaps no two single softball players have ever hated each other more than Hudson Swann and Snake Wingate. Snake Wingate is a player so mean, so ruthless that he is rumored to have a personally autographed picture of Don Sutton.

The Lizards are known from Cape Henry to Rehoboth Beach for their total lack of sportsmanship, and when the Jimmies play them, they're no charmers either, come to think of it. The field was littered with gobs of spit, balls of tar, and emery boards, and that was only some of the stuff the fans had thrown from the stands.

As Hudson stepped up to the plate, he was hoping that no one could see he was sweating doughballs. Snake was on a streak, no doubt about that. Hudson met his beady-eyed gaze with an expressive projectile of sunflower hulls and hated him even more than normal.

Not naturally introspective, Hudson realized that the entire town was watching him with interest and that if he blew this one, he could count on a lifetime as a social pariah. This, he decided, was one of those Big Moments life dishes out from time to time.

Thoughtfully, Hudson adjusted his cap, spat some more sunflower hulls, and gripped his Louisville Slugger in hands that he hoped were not shaking. Flakes of cork floated on the air around him.

Snake pulled his cap farther down over the place on his bald spot where his tarball was concealed and wound into a fastball that streaked past Hudson's bat.

"Strike one," said the ump, after some consultation with his seeing eye dog.

The crowd growled. Snake grinned and did a little dance on the mound. His Wingo groupies cheered him.

Hudson frowned, feeling the sweat pouring down his back. He gripped his bat even tighter, keeping his eye on Snake as the meanest player in the Micro Brewery League went through a dramatic series of contortions and let fly with another one of his patented fastballs. Hudson swung, feeling the ball sail just over his bat and into the catcher's mitt with a soft thud.

"Strike two," the ump yawned.

Wingo went wild; a shower of beer cans, old hot dog buns, and barbecue chicken bones rained down on the field.

Snake took it as his due, grinning at his fellow townsmen. "Heh, heh, heh," he said.

Hudson spread his feet, took his stance.

Snake wound up to pitch again.

The only sound was the buzzing of mosquitoes being fried in the bug zappers as the crowd held its breath.

Twirling his arm around like a bolo, Snake was thinking how good that Micro Brewery League Trophy would look behind the Jack Daniels bottles on the Dew Drop Inn bar down in Wingo. Using all of his strength and a little tar, he threw a fast curveball.

The Lizard fans were hauling out the cold duck.

Snake's ball flew from the mound in a long and evil arc.

Hudson pulled the Slugger back, then cracked forward.

The ball had not even reached him yet. He swung at thin air. But the momentum was so great that it swung Hudson all the way around in a 360-degree circle.

He connected with the ball on his way back.

Hudson only had time to watch the ball sail over the stands and into the Oysterback Hardshell Methodist Church graveyard before he took off, in a hail of cork dust, around the bases.

It is rumored that Snake Wingate quietly moved to West Virginia in the middle of the night, but Hudson thinks he'll be back for the playoffs.

We Was All Right, Huddie

We was all right, Huddie, I swear we was. Wade and Mookie and I only had about seven, eight beers apiece. Besides, it wasn't *our* fault that Wade had the gun. He'd just bought it offen a guy down the road and hadn't finished up the paperwork on it, that's all. It wasn't *really* concealed, he had it stuck in his *belt*. You just couldn't see it when the cops pulled him offen the truck 'cause his jacket fell down over it. They was no call to throw him up against the door like that, and that's what I told the judge, too.

Hell, all we was gonna do was go bass fishin' over to Tom's pond up to Windy Hill, but we got over to Tom's and his old lady told us not to go fishin' there because they had a whole bunch of *swans* layin' around the pond, and they didn't want 'em all riled up. You know what swans is like when they gets all riled up and they're nestin'? I knew you did, I was *with* you that time back up to Dunn's Cove when you had to beat that ole buck swan off with an oar. That scar never did heal up, did it?

Well, hell, Huddie, we was all right, I *swear*. We just had a coupla twelve-packs and them coupla joints of Mookie's, and we hadn't even smoked them yet when we decided that if we couldn't fish over to Tom's pond, we'd go on down to the Cove and see what we could do for ourselves. I mean, we weren't *drunk* or nothin'. We only had eight, ten beers apiece and Mookie ain't supposed to drink at all because he's still takin' them antibiotics after that other thing with Crystal, so he had them joints on him, but it were only a little weed. We was all right, Huddie.

Of course, it wasn't *our* fault that Wade hadda take a pee, was it? I mean, *everyone* knows, you don't buy beer, you just rent it, right? I mean, we was all right. So we was on the way to the Cove in Mookie's monster truck, and it was, like, one, two in the morning by then, so we figured what could it hurt to stop behind the View 'n' Chew so Wade could *relieve* hisself? I mean it was closed, nobody's gonna be looking for a sub and a video at two in the morning, are they? I mean, we was all right, Huddie, ya know?

So, ole Wade and Mookie, they just hop on down outta the truck and let loose next to the recycling barrels and the *next* thing you know, there's about twenty-eleven cops and spotlights and mari-ja-wana-sniffin' dogs and I'm lookin' down the barrel of a po-lice Special .38. I mean, Huddie, we was all right. Except for the beer cans Mookie put down, I mean he didn't *throw* them down or nothing, out of the truck, on the asphalt next to the recycling barrels. And Wade hollers out, "I gotta gun in my belt, you'd better take it out," but I guess they didn't hear the last part, but you *know* ole Wade wouldn't hurt nobody, lessen it was that common sorry jerk what hit on Tawnee over at the Epics Lounge that time, but there Mookie was, caught, so to speak, in mid-stream, surrounded by all these cops a-whoopin' and a-hollerin' and a-goin' on all 'bout how we was these here big-time crack dealers and we was in a whole, serious *world* of deep doo, that they'd been stakin' out behind the View 'n' Chew for weeks—I just threw my head back and laughed, because *everyone* knows that Wade and Mookie can't even get it together between the two of 'em to buy a case o' Red, White an' Blue, let alone that there crack stuff. I mean, them people what owns the View 'n' Chew's so born again, they don't even sell *cigarettes*. I mean, we was in the middle of a stakeout! I mean, them crack dealers is all over to Wallopsville, *everyone* knows that. That's when *I* got confused. But we was all right, Mookie and Wade and me, even with a gun and some pot and them there beer cans. And you know Mookie, he had to get some attitude, then Wade jumps in, and I'm saying "Shut up, Mookie" and then—well, *you* know. It just got real weird, but *we* was all right.

I disremember what happened after that too much, but as is usual, the Mookster and Wade-man and me was in the wrong place at the wrong time, but we *was* all right, by the time you got there. Just a few charges, and the judge gave us probation before judgment, so we was all right.

It's *everyone else* that's nuts around here, if you ast me.

Desiree and Earl Don Rekindle the Magic

Since Helga and Poot Wallop are visiting her sister Fern's family in their RV park in Ocean View, I, Desiree Grinch, proprietor of the Blue Crab Tavern, promised I would get out this edition of the *Bugeye*. The trouble is, I am no writer, no matter what Miss Wimbleforth, my tenth-grade English teacher, said, but I have to finish up this copy so I can rush it down to Kinko's in time for the deathline, or whatever Helga calls it.

Anyway, I guess since everyone knows what happened with the FBI agent, the albino crab, and Ferrus T. Buckett, the only thing left to tell you all about is that my ex, Earl Don Grinch, and I had a date last night and went over to the new mall in Salisbury to the movies after we had steaks at the Pine Ridge. It is always good to eat someone else's cooking, I told Earl Don, especially by citronella candlelight, so don't get any funny ideas.

I was hoping he would take me to see something romantic like *Ghost,* which is a love story about dead Patrick Swayze, especially after I saw page 75 of *People* magazine, but I should have known after four years of marriage to that man that Earl Don can no more resist one of those pictures where everyone is armed and dangerous and blowing everyone else up in high-speed car chases than I can pass up anything with Elvis on it.

I think the name of the movie we went to see was Total Blowhard II, with that German who married that Kennedy girl, but I was so steamed that Earl Don actually had the nerve to steer me past the Harrison Ford picture next door that I wasn't paying much attention.

"Earl Don," I said, "if I want to see high-speed car chases and people shooting each other, I may as well go home and sit on the deck in Oysterback, because I don't charge three dollars for a cup of watered-down diet soda." But you know Earl Don; once that man has an idea in his head, you can't change him, so we went to see the blood-and-guts movie with Bruce Swartzenwillis or whoever, the one with the muscles.

Anyway, we went in and actually found two seats together, which was a miracle, since that itty-bitty theater was packed to the gills, and we sat down. Well, you know Earl Don; give him something bright and loud that moves and he's gone to the world, and that's why Huddie and Junie were able to sneak in that night and blow up the lava lamp the way they did, but right away, all I heard was these people behind us.

They were talking, right loud, about some relation of theirs named Poor Gloria, and believe me, what happened to Poor Gloria shouldn't have happened to a dog. I'll tell Poor Gloria, wherever she is, that I'd just as soon have a quadruple bypass like she did than sit in a movie theater and listen to my relatives rake my character over the coals the way they were, while that muscleman was blowing people's heads off right up there on the screen.

Well, then I noticed this strange but familiar smell, and after a while I realized that the guy next to me, who must have been forty if he was a day, was wearing enough Polio cologne to stink out a mourner's bench. I am willing to bet you that every waterman between New Church and Havre de Grace got a bottle of Polio cologne for Christmas last year, because every time they put off their gumboots and take a shower, you can smell them downwind of a seafood plant.

I guess it attracted something, because he was sitting there with his arm around a girl young enough to be his daughter with a mall do that she must have constructed with Elmer's. You know that pouf, that roll of hair those girls get going out from their foreheads? Well, this child's pouf was about eight inches long and stood up with a life of its own.

Every time she turned her head, she was scraping the whiskers off her old daddy boyfriend, and him trying to sneak a kiss like he was a teenager. Earl Don says men like firm flesh and soft minds, but I have yet to discover what these girls want with these wasted old yobbos who weren't even interesting when they were back in high school. I guess it's just one of those things, but when I catch those old boys after the little girls in the Blue Crab, I remind 'em that I knew 'em when they had hair.

Well, between all the details of Poor Gloria's bypass, and what her husband was doing while she was in the hospital, and the cologne and the mall do, I never did find out what was plaguing Clint Swartzen-willis, but just as Poor Gloria's husband was about to be caught out wearing Poor Gloria's L. L. Bean flannel nightie by Miss Lucinda, whoever she might be, old Earl Don leaned over to me and started to sing "Heartbreak Hotel."

Well, Earl Don hasn't done that since the magic went out of our marriage five years ago, so I was right touched and suggested we head for our favorite parking spot down by the cove.

As we were leaving, I saw this woman come in, and I just knew that she hadn't come to see the movie. She had her eyes narrow and she was a-sniffing of the air like she was looking for a whiff of Polio, and I just sort of shuffled Earl Don out of there before she found her man with the mall do young enough to be his daughter. Earl Don hates confrontation.

Don't you just hate it when the audience is more interesting than the movie?

Even a Jonah Can Have a Piece of Luck

He had done everything he could think of to do, and the damned engine still wouldn't turn over. Worse, while he'd been fiddling with it, trying to get it cranked up again, the workboat had been drifting steadily away from his lay and in toward shore. With a nudge, her bow hit mud bottom twenty feet from the bank, and the *June Debbie* gave a little sigh, as if she were saying, "Well, what do you expect?"

Junior Redmond, in the throes of a run of bad luck, expected nothing. He merely cursed, slamming the lid back down on the engine box, glaring into the cuddy, where the radio rankled with static. He had sent out a call for a tow, and he hoped that some waterman, coming in late, might have heard him and even now be heading toward Log Cabin Point and his eventual rescue. But, being a philosophical type, he didn't expect too much. Off to the west, the setting sun was obscured by black and evil-looking thunderheads, pregnant with rain and lightning. The storm was moving toward him.

With a sigh, Junie unrolled his unfiltered Camels from his T-shirt sleeve, watching as his lighter slid through his greasy fingers, bounced on the washboard and sailed over the side of the boat, disappearing into the water with a solid plunk.

Experience had taught him that when a man is in the throes of a spell of being a Jonah, the best thing to do is wait it out, just as, when a man is on a roll, the best thing to do is take every advantage. Such are the seasons of change.

Junie reached into the ice chest and pulled out a can of Vienna sausages. He did not even wince when he laid his finger open on the lid, merely wiping his bloody thumb on his pants.

The first drops of rain splattered across the boards as he thoughtfully munched on a Vienna sausage, swatting at the mosquitoes swarming around his face.

Save for the restless clawing of the crabs in the bushel baskets, uneasily sensing the coming storm, it was still. The water lay flat, without so much as a ripple; no wind stirred through the pines on the shore, and not so much as a mockingbird sang in the soybean field beyond.

As Junie munched his sausages, he watched the storm darkness gather over the twilight, and heard the distant rumble of thunder over Calvert Cliffs, across the Bay.

The radio squealed and died, the static fading to nothingness.

It was still, too still, he thought, spearing a Vienna sausage with his Buck knife. He knew he was going to have indigestion later, but his other choice was a mouldy packet of Little Debbie Devil Dogs one of the kids had shoved under the charts on the rising beam last August.

The thunder, having rumbled, was silent.

Splatters of rain fell on the boat, on Junie's neck and shoulders. The rain felt cool on his skin, and he lifted his face to the gray skies.

Having finished the last sausage, he tossed the can into a compound bucket and lifted the top off the engine box again, as if, refreshed, he could now divine the problem he had been unable to fathom all afternoon. Like the shade-tree mechanic he knew himself to be, Junie fiddled with the battery wires again, as if a jiggle would work, then eased forward to pull an oar out from the cuddy.

Standing up on the washboard, he began to rock the *June Debbie* loose from the mud; with a sucking sound, she shifted off, afloat, free on the shallow water.

At that moment, there was a terrible cracking sound, as if the very skies themselves had broken apart, and for a second the whole world was illuminated in white light.

Blinded, Junie took a step backward, gripping the shaft of the oar for support.

The stillness that followed was even more eerie than the silence that had preceded the lightning strike. After a brief mental assessment to be certain that he had not been struck by the bolt, Junie shifted in his gumboots and whistled through his teeth. As soon as his ears stopped ringing, he noticed another, familiar sound, and realized that his engine was running again.

As best as a shade-tree mechanic could figure, the jump from the blue had struck his radio antenna, traveled through the wire and charged the battery. Or something like that. His radio was beyond repair, but the big old Ford Marine V-8 was purring as if she had just been tuned up.

The Redmonds were a race bred not to question the vagaries of chance. Throwing the throttle into medium, Junie backed off the mud shoal and pointed *June Debbie*'s bow toward the channel, making for the harbor before the rain.

Briefly, he considered what the tale would tell like down at the Blue Crab, then dismissed it. No one would believe him anyway. His Jonah, he assumed, was over, but he was not about to make a test case of it.

To Sleep, Perchance to Dream

There's a spring moon out tonight, as full and yellow as one of Miss Nettie Leery's oyster fritters, and it's hanging in the sky, right above Oysterback.

Beneath the glittering surface of the Devanaux River and out among the grasses in Widgeon Marsh, the world is alive and moving. In the light of the full moon, things are out there fighting, eating, killing and mating, dying and being born, and the night is full of their sounds.

Over at the edge of the old burial ground at Oysterback Hardshell Methodist Church, an eighteen-point buck, the exact same buck that Junie Redmond has been pursuing for years, is grazing on new forsythia shoots, one eye on his harem of does and their fawns, the other peeled for trouble.

Out on the river, a single skate, the size of a kitchen table top, breaks the surface of the cold and sparkling water, plunging back again into the silent depths.

In Oysterback, the humans, and most of the dogs and cats too, are sleeping.

Some have just gone to bed an hour ago, like Desiree Grinch, who has closed up the tavern and fallen asleep in the middle of David Letterman, buried in her yellow satin comforter, dreaming of Elvis being alive and well and in the federal witness-protection program, running a topless bar in Cambridge. In the morning, she will not remember this dream.

Others will be getting up in an hour or so, while the moon is still riding low in the sky and dawn is just a thought on the horizon.

Hudson Swann, soaked with cold sweat, dreams—again—that he is back in Quon Tre with his platoon, talking to Tavlik, who is walking beside him, when there is a sudden crack, and suddenly, where Tavlik's head was before, there is a spurting, bloody stump. Hudson opens his mouth to scream and awakens, sitting upright in bed, staring into the moonlight, his wife asleep beside him, his daughters asleep down the hall, and he knows he will have this dream for the rest of his life.

In the dark and heavy bed in which he was conceived, and his father before him, Parsons Dreedle smacks his lips, dreaming of Mrs. Ella

Sparks's lemon custard pie, high as a featherbed, as sweet and tangy as the first bite of, well, as Mrs. Ella Sparks's lemon custard pie.

In her dreams, Mrs. Carlotta Hackett is eighteen again, and riding on the Oysterback Volunteer Fire Department truck, waving to the crowds as she relives the most glorious moment of her life.

Junie Redmond snores loudly, but in his dreams he is swinging from the rigging of a fine old Spanish galleon, as swashbuckling a pirate as ever sailed the Spanish Main, engaged in hand-to-hand combat with Blackbeard. Guess who's winning?

Miss Nettie Leery, hair wrapped carefully in tissue, sleeps alone as she has slept since the death of Alva Leery fifteen years ago. But in her dream, Alva is alive again, pulling on his socks and shoes as he sits in the bedroom chair and looks out the window, remarking on the pair of bluebirds who have started to build a nest in the privet hedge down by the shed this year. Even in her sleep, Miss Nettie knows this is a dream, but she hangs on to it as long as she can.

Down at the harbor, rocked by the tide, Professor Shepherd sleeps in his boat, dreaming that he is delivering a lecture on pathetic fallacies in the novels of the Victorians to the Baltimore Orioles.

No one knows what Ferrus T. Buckett dreams of, down at the end of Black Dog Road in his old shanty. But there is a smile on his face, and he dreams in perfect Parisian French.

Fried Chicken and the Religious Right

"**N**ow," says Miss Nettie, "I call this nice." She settles herself down at the picnic table and looks around at the assembled faces. Most of them aren't looking at her; they're all fixated on the big platter of her fried chicken she's placed in the middle of the table, between the sliced tomatoes and the Silver Queen corn. Miss Nettie's fried chicken is the stuff dreams are made of.

Even Reverend Briscoe is in the spirit of things; he makes the grace short and sweet. "Bless this fried—ahem, this *food*—to Thy service, Lord, amen," he says, and he's rewarded with the first breast off the plate and an extra large spoonful of Ella Sparks's potato salad.

"You know, Reverend," Doreen Redmond says to him, teasing, "I never did yet see a minister that didn't like fried chicken." Quick like, she reaches over and smacks her youngest kid's hand out of the roll basket. "They will be passed to you, Chelsea," she says.

Surely, there will be Miss Nettie's fried chicken in heaven.

"Well, there's one minister who'll never eat another bite," Junior Redmond says, and sort of grins at his best friend Hudson Swann. But Huddie's about to have a big bite of a chicken thigh, and he just shakes his head.

"That's Reverend Briscoe's story. He ought to tell it," Huddie says. "You and I were just there, sort of."

Well, it only takes a little coaxing, but Reverend Alfred Briscoe likes a good story as much as any Eastern Shoreman, so he takes a sip from his iced tea and clears his throat.

"A while back, recall, I had a visit from a classmate from my seminary, Billy Sol Gantry."

"The TV preacher?" Desiree Grinch asks. "The one that says the Equal Rights Amendment is a 'communist plot to destroy the American family and turn women into children-killing, husband-leaving lesbians who plan to destroy capitalism through the use of witchcraft, but they won't, if you put your hand on the TV and send him money for his $600 suits?'" There is a dangerous edge in her voice.

"He was hidin' out after that scandal with the topless duchess," Junie

snorted, helping himself to another cat's-head biscuit. "Huddie and I could see that ole Billy Sol was makin' the Rev unhappy, braggin' about his big ole rich tee-vee ministry and how he was rakin' in the Cadillacs and the big Republican checks, so we figured we'd take him out fishing, get him out of Rev's hair for a while, right? Well, lo and behold, ole Billy Sol Gantry there hooked a great big ole blue, and while he was reeling it in, his whole set of false teeth, them great big white shiny choppers you see on TV, they come outta his mouth and fell in the water. Out to Jack's Hole, where it's about three hundred feet deep, no less."

Junie and Huddie are both looking suspiciously innocent, as if they had nothing to do with this. Huddie even picks up the story here.

"Well, that was fine with us, we was tired a listenin' to him inflate himself. And you know you ain't gonna find *nothin'* once it's gone down Jack's Hole. But Reverend here, he prevailed on us to do the Christian thing and try to retrieve Billy Sol's store teeth.

"So, we grabbed up one of Miss Nettie here's fried chicken legs, and we tied it to a long, long string and dropped it overboard into Jack's Hole.

"And lo and behold, after a bit, we get a bite, and we reel that long string up, and there's Billy Sol's teeth, grippin' on that chicken leg like it was their last hope of salvation, which it well might have been.

"Billy Sol left town right after that. I guess facin' the media about the topless duchess was easier than admitting that no preacher can resist Miss Nettie's chicken," Huddie said, reaching for another piece.

"Maybe that'll teach him to bad-mouth women," Desiree says. "And witches," she adds under her breath with a small, strange smile.

OYSTERBACK ✳ BUGEYE

● *Published Every Now and Then Or Whenever There's News* ●
Helga Wallop, Editor. ✍ PO BOX 3, OYSTERBACK MD, 210000 Price ✚ 25 cents.

MOSQUITO FESTIVAL IS BIG HIT !

Aliens from Uranus Invade New York

What's News from the *Oysterback Bugeye:*
Entertainment News from Our Hometown Paper

Bugeye *editor Helga Wallop's thoughts: "I'm the town gossip anyway; I may as well get paid for it".*

• • •

MORE THAN A HUNDRED PEOPLE attended the Seventeenth Annual Oysterback Mosquito Festival this month, breaking all records for attendance. *Musca* lovers from as far away as Belize and Equatorial Africa came to celebrate the Eastern Shore's State Bird and to share the fun of Mosquito Swats and competitions for the Biggest Skeeter, Biggest Bugbite, and Best Imitation of an Annoying Mosquito Whine. As always, the highlight of the Festival was Thursday night's Mosquito Race, when entries from Maine, Maryland, Florida, and Louisiana competed to be the first to find and bite an expanse of human flesh. Special thanks to Joey Buttafuoco, this year's Celebrity Host, for being the finish line for all those hungry skeeters. Congrats to this year's winner Lamont L'Eureux, from Cou de Rouge, LA, with his winning skeeter, Miss Budweiser. *C'est la guerre,* Joey; hope you heal up soon!

• • •

IN OTHER SHOW BIZ NEWS, don't forget the big dance recital over to Patti's Christian School of Tap and Ballet, Saturday at two over to Wallopsville. Crystal Tiffany Tutweiler, 16, will be doing her tap interpretations of "Teenage Girls in the Old Testament."

• • •

AND IN YET MORE entertainment news, did everyone remember to tune in "Southern Sportsman" last weekend? If you looked real close you could just see Alonzo Deaver drum fishing off Cape Charles for about five seconds. He was on the head boat right behind Franc White, when Franc was holding up that big red drum and talking about lures. We hear Paisley Redmond caught the show; he recognized his missing tackle that disappeared from his boat last spring. No court date has been set, but that was a nice recipe for lemon pepper bluefish Franc did at the end of the show, so watch for reruns.

• • •

IN MORE FISHING NEWS, the Oysterback Bass-O-Rama Tournament is coming up this month, so get your entry forms now. Catch-and-release fishermen should be at Dodd's Pond no later than eight o'clock. To prevent mishaps like last year's, this year's tourney has been rescheduled so as to not interfere with the swans' nesting season.

• • •

TRY-OUTS FOR "GUYS AND DOLLS" at the Oysterback Community Theater are starting next week. Don't forget to come on down and watch Hagar Jump snap up a big role like she does every year. She thinks Sky Masterson is a woman's part, and some people hope no one tells her any different, if they know what's good for them.

• • •

OYSTERBACK SENIOR CITIZENS CENTER will be sponsoring a bus trip to Lollapalooza on the thirtieth. Seniors who wish to go are asked to bring a box lunch, comfortable shoes, and their favorite Eurotech music tapes. See or call Venus Tutweiler for details.

• • •

HELGA WALLOP, editor of this paper and Oysterback's artist in residence, will be giving a craft lesson at the Community Center next week. Anyone who wishes to make a handy and useful toilet paper roll doll cover should bring an empty soda bottle, a rag, and a cup of gasoline. Unleaded, please. We're concerned about our environment!

• • •

THE REVERSE GEAR PICKUP TRUCK Mud Bogs, usually held in Elwood Rainbird's pig lot on Patamoke Seafood's payday after last call, have been moved to Captain Lennie Skinner's pasture because of last week's hurricane. Lennie says bring cash.

• • •

OYSTERBACK WAS MILDLY CURIOUS last week when Hollywood movie star Jeremy Jason was in town shooting scenes for his new movie, *The Hooley Legume Story,* about Oysterback's only native major league ballplayer. Residents were quick to exclaim over the presence of the somewhat famous actor, who ate lunch at the Blue Crab Tavern on Tuesday with members of the crew. He ordered a cheeseburger, fries, and a Coke, it was reported, and acted "pretty normal," according to waitress Beth Redmond. Johnny Ray, who was in the men's room at the same time the actor was at the Gas 'n' Go, says he's got a tattoo. Omar Hinton reports that Jeremy bought a package of Sun Chips, a package of wintergreen Lifesavers, and a sour cherry Sundance during a break in the filming on Thursday and admired the stuffed chicken hawk over the store counter. "Not too many foreigners like that old thing," Omar reports. "Mostly they come in, look at it, and wince." The crew stayed at Inez Bugg's bed and breakfast over in Patamoke, rented a couple of movies from the View 'n' Chew, shot scenes in and around Widgeon Marsh and the softball field, and didn't have any wild Hollywood sex or do any drugs that anyone will admit to. Anyone who wants to see the autograph that Hagar Jump, Oysterback's postmaster, got can look at the bulletin board down at the post office during regular hours. "It's for my niece," Hagar says. Right.

Desiree Meets the God of Excess

I guess because I, Desiree Grinch, proprietor of the Blue Crab Tavern, dragged her there, Helga Wallop went into Salisbury to the new mall to see the Jimmy Velvet Traveling Elvis Museum and Mike El, the Elvis impersonator that my friend Delores up in Havre de Grace saw at the Conowingo Inn. Helga likes Elvis all right, but she's not a hard-core fan, so she said I had to write it all up for the *Bugeye* because she couldn't begin to do justice to it.

The Jimmy Velvet Traveling Elvis Museum was really something. They had one of Elvis's Cadillacs, and a whole lot of his jewelry and clothes and stuff in these plastic cases. I particularly liked the watch Elvis designed himself that flashes a Star of David and a Cross every twenty seconds because it showed Elvis was really interested in religion and spiritual values, even if he did take all those pills.

I also enjoyed all of Elvis's belts and buckles and so forth that looked like he was a wrestling champion, and Helga said, "Well, no one can accuse the man of having any taste," and I told her to shush, because this big lady with white-blonde hair was standing next to us touching the case with his Christmas card of Graceland, looking all lit up like it was under siege by a SWAT team, and she was crying soundlessly and you knew she was a real Elvis fan and this was a magic moment for her.

I was wondering how they accumulated all this Elvisiana when I noticed that everything was authenticated with a little card signed by some friend of Elvis's saying the King had given it to them. Then I knew, I mean, it is very bad taste to give away a gift, and I still have that "Chad Everett Sings the Beatles" album Miss Nettie gave me in the church round robin last year when she was my Sunshine Sister, so you sort of wonder what kind of friends Elvis must have had who could sell the gifts he had given them.

Well, I got into a talk with Kathy Velvet, Jimmy's wife, who takes this museum all over the country, from mall to mall for forty weeks a year, and she was very nice. I bought a porcelain bell with a picture of Elvis in "Clambake" on it for my collection, and Helga got one of the T-shirts with a picture of the King on it that look like black velvet

paintings. She says she's going to make Poot wear it, but I've never seen Poot wear anything but those Mexican sport shirts.

So anyway, then it was time to go down to the Food Court and see the Mike El show. My friend Delores, the nurse in Havre de Grace, had Mike El in the hospital with knee surgery, and she said he was Elvis the whole time he was in there, silk pajamas and all, so I have been dying to see him. His name is Michael, but he calls himself Mike El, I guess in tribute to the King.

She later saw him at the Conowingo Inn, and she said it was a pretty good show for a guy from Aberdeen, but I said well, he can't be any worse than Tonto Snavely was when he was doing his Elvis impersonation at the Waterman's Convention in Ocean City last January. You have not lived until you have seen an Elvis-impersonating waterman, but that is another story.

Well, he doesn't look like Elvis, so I guess he hasn't had plastic surgery or anything, and Helga said he looked just like Poot doing an Elvis impression, so I had to tell her to hush, but he stood up there with what I think was the Blue Heaven Band and shook his butt, which was draped with all these chains, all over the place, and there were about a thousand little old redneck ladies in there and they just all swooned and took on something fierce.

He had this girl who was probably his daughter handing him these red Arnel scarves, and he would sing and drape them around his neck, then hand them out to the little old redneck ladies in the audience. After a while these little kids would come up to the stage, and he would hand out scarves to the little girls, which was real cute, I thought. Then he came down into the audience and sang to the ladies, and when he got up on top of us, I thought maybe I would get a scarf, but Helga reached out and jerked one of the chains on his butt.

Well, there was quite a scene, and I almost lost my porcelain bell, but one of the security guards, a real cute one, said he'd meet us over to Dockside Murphy's later, and he did. We didn't get in till about one in the morning, and Poot and Earl Don were furious but not as furious as I was at Helga for jerking Mike El's chains. Naturally I would never go back there for another show, but Helga says it doesn't matter since he only sings the real God of Excess late-model stuff, not the great stuff like "Heartbreak Hotel" or "Blue Christmas." "But I'll give him this," Helga said, "he's got a great sense of showmanship."

I'm just mad that she got one of those red Arnel scarves and I didn't.

The Midnight Waterman Escort Service

I don't imagine I have to tell you things are bad. You probably have your own way of gauging hard times, but for me it's the pot of deer-meat chili I keep on the stove all winter for those that need to eat. The faster that pot goes down, the worse things are, and lately that pot's been awful damn low.

But we had an idea the other day we like. See what you think.

It was a usual Wednesday Girls' Night when we were sitting around the bar waiting for the Lotto drawing. Some of us had tickets; none of us had high hopes, except Hagar Jump, Oysterback's postmaster, who bought about ten tickets based on some new system that uses logarithms and her grandchildren's birthdays. Hagar is an eternal optimist, while I, Desiree Grinch, proprietor of the Blue Crab Tavern, tend to move more in the other direction.

Miss Nettie Leery sort of summed up the general mood when she looked up from her pink squirrel she'd been nursing all night and said, "I lived through the Great Depression and a world war and I have never seen anything this bad."

"It's the dermo and the PMS that killed all the oysters," Doreen Redmond sighed, stroking her lottery tickets against the bar.

"MSX," Jeanne Swann said absently, watching the sports wrap-up on Channel 16, over the bar. "My daddy always used to say 'Well, you can get a job over to the wire factory,' but they're laying off too, now."

"If we don't get some crabs this summer, you're gonna see a lot of people leavin' this marsh come fall. Business is 'way off down to the Salon de Beaute," Doreen sighed.

"I'm right tired of Tuna Helper," Helga put in. "And it's three days till the Social Security checks come in."

"I told Junie if things don't get any better, I'm gonna rent him out," Doreen said, laughing. "Some of the weekender ladies who come into the Salon de Beaute say, 'Oh, my, Doreen, it must be nice to be married to an outdoors man instead of my boring old lawyer or stockbroker, so neurotic and selfish.' At least Junie doesn't sit on the edge of the bed and say he can't see you the same day he sees his therapist." She took a sip from her screwdriver.

"That's fine if you like being around a guy who can only deal with his feelings about dogs or moving engine parts," I said. "You can follow them from room to room going, 'how do you feel about, oh, you know, whatever's going on at the moment,' and they panic and lock themselves in the bathroom. A nice, rich, selfish stockbroker looks good to me right now, especially if he can help me make the mortgage."

"I'll have you know," Helga says, mocking a man's voice, "that there are a lot of women who would be thrilled to go out with us here fine upstanding Oysterback men. Some of us clean up real good and even know what fork to use. Why, Huddie has his own black tie!"

"And white boots," Jeanne cried. "Would you all be thinking of taking Huddie to a white boot affair or a black boot affair?"

"We could call it the Midnight Waterman Escort Service," Doreen said, opening a bag of miniature Snickers bars and passing them around. "We'll provide you with a macho outdoors man of your choice. With or without teeth, in Ferrus's case."

"Boy, can you imagine those bored, rich, urban, yuppie women snapping them right up? They look at Huddie in his old tight jeans and that cute butt and you can see them drooling," Jeanne laughed. "And he's had two years of college, although you wouldn't know it to look at him."

"Wait till Parsons Dreedle has a couple of drinks and starts quoting Robert Service to them!" Helga giggled. "That would certainly be a change from policy wonking."

"Tired of endless conversations about *him, him, HIM?* Try a man who communicates in a series of sophisticated grunts!"

Well, all men, inside or outside the beltways, do that. But we still think it's a good idea, so if you are interested in the Midnight Waterman Escort Service, come down to Oysterback. We have 'em in all colors, shapes, ages, sizes, and testosterone levels. Just come by the Blue Crab on Girls' Night and we'll fix you right up.

Especially that lady up in Baltimore who won the Lotto.

Sysco Man—
EGGS
BUTTER BALLS
FRITOLAY
6 CHIPS
8 PEANUTS

POOL TABLE
ORDER
PLAY OFFS
1. H.   FERRUS
2. J.   VS
3. F.   DMitir

Call J.C. Dodd
re: LITES
Earl Don- car Keys
for
bowling
tonight

7:00

Blue Crab Tavern

Oysterback, Maryland
Desiree Grinch, proprietor

☆☆☆☆- *Guide Michelin*

DOREEN—
c. Veg cup .75
Jemie cup o.s. 75
Pick up
NOON

WEDNESDAY'S SPECIALS

‖ THH	Crab Vegetable Soup bowl $1.50 cup .75
THH	Cream of Crab Soup bowl $1.50 cup .75
‖‖	Oyster Stew bowl $1.50 cup .75
‖‖	Corn Soup market price
‖‖	Muskrat Stew w/Okra $4.95
	Fried Muskrat Sandwich $3.95
‖	Oyster Fritters $4.95

~~Bluefish Desirée market price~~ SOLD OUT

Beth's Burger $3.50

Beth's Special Burger $4.50

Vegetarian Corn Salad $2.50

Comes with choice of fries,hot potato salad,cole slaw
or lemon-ginger pickle.

Beth—6 hrs Wed.
5 hr Thur
6 hr Fri
17 HRS.

886
5100

Harlequin Surprise Jello Mold $1.00 — again next week?
Chocolate Fudge Pecan Death $2.50
Hot Apple Pie and Cheddar $1.50
~~Ginger Pumpkin Cake~~ $1.50 SOLD OUT

Ask about Junie Redmond's 7 Course Special-
A six pack of Buds and a crab cake sandwich
to go...only $5.00

JUNIE *we do not serve unpleasant people*

O's $2.00 to me. for 2 Buds Longnecks

Junie Redmond's Day in Court

J ust by the way that his black robes flapped about him like the wings of an angry crow, regulars in Judge Findlay Fish's courtroom could tell that he was in one of his black moods as he sailed in, taking his seat on the bench.

The line between his bushy eyebrows was as deep as the Baltimore Canyon, and the assistant state's attorney, a young woman with the ink not yet quite dry on her law degree, stuck her Nicorette under the table as she exchanged a meaningful look with the bailiff. The judge grunted as he rifled through his docket, and the crier ordered the spectators to be seated.

Junior Redmond was, in his own way, something of a regular in this bile-yellow room, and he tried to sink down into his sport coat, his Christmas tie bunching painfully under his freshly shaved neck as he attempted to become invisible. His one consolation so far was that that most efficient of Fish Cops, Lt. Louisa Kelsey, had not yet appeared in court. His worst fear was that Hudson Swann would not show up in time. It was $300 or thirty days, and Huddie had been assigned to collect the money in cash before Junie's case came before the bench.

Junie knew Judge Fish, and he had heard the inside gossip that the judge had been lecturing no-show jurors this morning, an activity designed to put him in the worst mood. A thirty-days-or-$300 sort of mood.

"I thought I told you never to show up in my courtroom again, Junie," the judge said in measured tones, glaring at the hapless waterman. "After that last episode with Uranians invading the Patamoke Seafood Plant, I thought you'd learned your lesson."

Junie grinned sickly, feeling a cold line of sweat break out on his spine. Judge Fish was in a mood to be all business today.

"It was a small rockfish, Judge," he said weakly.

All he got for his trouble was a baleful look; behind his glasses, the judge's eyes looked like twin nooses to Junie, and he recalled, without pleasure, the smell of the Santimoke Detention Center, a mixture of fear, sweat, and unwashed bodies.

As Junie watched the clock crawling away the morning, Judge Fish dealt summarily with nonsupporting fathers, a DWI appeal, and a crack dealer's sentencing. Usually, putting a drug dealer away for an extended period of time would put the judge in a better mood, but not today. His face was still all long lines and hard looks when Junior heard his own name being called.

He looked at the door, then at the clock; it was almost noon and still no Hudson, no $300.

As he approached the bench, Junior heard a deep, dark, rumbling sound. At first, he thought it was a car starting up on the street outside, but then he realized it was Judge Fish's stomach. Dressing down the no-show jurors had deprived him of his breakfast, and now he was anxious to have done and get on to the lunch recess. How the judge's stomach complained!

Junior Redmond would be the first to admit that inspiration rarely seizes him but that when it does, it seizes him good.

"Well, Judge," he said, "it was like this. When they put the ban on rockfish, it hurt. It hurt where I live. There's nothing in this world like a rock, all grilled on a slow flame and served up on a plate, with just a smidge of salt and pepper, a dab of butter, the way that white, fine fish just flakes away on your fork, melts in your mouth . . ."

The judge was looking interested. Hungry, but interested.

Junie plunged on, lowering his voice so that just the young state's attorney and the judge could hear him, as if he were telling a naughty tale. "Oh, down to Oysterback, we tried. We had perch, fried with just a little onion in a red hot skillet, we had flounder with green peppercorns, we had shad roe, baked against an open fire on a plank, so that the salt just pops out of the eggs in your mouth like an explosion.

"We had crab meat. Crab salads, all pink, crab cakes—well, judge, you've never missed a supper at Oysterback Hardshell Methodist Church, you know what an Oysterback crab cake is like, how it just melts in your mouth . . . but there's nothing quite the same as a bite of that fine, fine rockfish.

"Well, I tried and I prayed and I sweated, and I did the right thing; ever' time I went fishing and I had one a them big striped beauties on my line, I cut it loose, watched it swim away, as if it were on my dinner plate with a side of Miss Nettie Leery's cottage fries and a dish of fried tomatoes . . ."

Junior sighed, shaking his head. The judge was looking at him as if he were a plate of food, and he would eat him up. The judicial stomach growled, demanding to be fed. If the Hon. Findlay Fish had less dignity, he would have drooled.

"Well, this went on for pret' near two years, Judge. I'd started to dream about rockfish at night, a nice tender white fillet, laying across the plate, and me just about to take a bite of it and raise it to my mouth when I'd wake up. Not even in my dreams could I experience rockfish, the best eating fish in the Bay.

"Well, finally, last September, when we was tonging, and it was such a nice day, I couldn't stand it no more. I put a line over, and when that fish come up, she was a rock. Just as pretty as you could stand, about eighteen inches long." Junie swallowed. It was more than a human being could stand, Judge! I was just about to toss 'er back over when Big Louisa pulled alongside."

The judge's empty stomach let out one last gurgling protest just as the door of the court slammed open and Hudson, a white bank packet in his hand, blinked around the room. The long hand of the clock met the small hand at the 12.

Like the sun behind thunderheads, Judge Fish's smile warmed the room. "Thirty days or $300," he said, rising from the bench. "Lunch recess!"

As Hudson placed the money in Junie's hands, he smiled. "Rockfish plate special over to the Elite Luncheonette today," he drawled.

It's Safer up Here

If she shifts a little and leans back against the trunk of the tree, Jeanne Swann can see all the way down past the soybean field to the river. Up here in the tree house, sheltered by leaves and protected from the world by dark blue night, she almost feels safe. Almost, but not quite. Ugly reality, like a hound from hell, seems to be lurking just below, waiting for her to come down. She fishes a cigarette out of the crumpled package and lights it, inhaling deeply. The patches aren't working. Nothing, it seems to her, is working these days.

In the dark, she can just see the thin white straps of her sandals wrapped around her ankles. She has always been proud of her feet, small and well shaped, always paid as much attention to her toes as her fingers.

While she doesn't hear her husband coming up the tree, she's not entirely surprised when Hudson's face appears, pale above his beard in the moonlight.

"What time is it?" Jeanne asks.

"About two-thirty," Hudson replies. The silence between them is not uncomfortable. He climbs up on the platform and settles awkwardly down opposite her. He's a big man, tall and thick, and he doesn't like small spaces high up off the ground.

"So?" he asks, after a while.

"It's safer up here," Jeanne says.

When it looks as if Hudson doesn't understand, and men are like that, Jeanne shakes her head. "I don't know what it is. Maybe it's the fact that people are so poor, and times are so hard, and there's no relief in sight, but I tell you, this is the Age of Irritability.

"Listen, honey, Doreen and Desiree had a big fight because Doreen doesn't approve of what she thinks is Desiree running that young boy, Michael, and then Carlotta Hackett was there getting her roots done and she jumped into it, and Desiree and Doreen turned on her, and she stormed out of the salon and backed into Faraday Hicks's pickup truck, and he told her she was mutton dressed as lamb, and when Faraday went into Omar Hinton's he was so mad he kicked Warner, Omar's dog, and Omar threw a price gun at his head.

"Only trouble was, he missed and hit your father square in the jaw and dislodged his upper plate, and Captain Hardee got so mad he went for Omar but he fell over Warner, who was lying in the middle of the floor, and knocked over the Little Debbie Snack Cakes display. My mother was over behind the Little Debbie Snack Cakes fetching a carton of milk down, and all those Devil Dogs got all over her Wednesday afternoon bridge dress, and now she's mad at your father *and* Faraday Hicks *and* Omar.

"Miss Nettie went on over to the Blue Crab to wash off that sticky chocolate stuff in the ladies' room, and Beth, who was tending bar, was having trouble with the baby and hadn't had a chance to clean out the toilets, so she told Mom the restrooms were for customers only, and Mom was so put out that she called Beth and Paisley's baby a no-neck brat and said all the Redmonds weren't worth the powder it would take to blow them to hell, and Beth, well, you know how sensitive these artistic types are, she burst into tears, and about that time Ferrus T. Buckett came in, hoping someone was there who would buy him a drink, and he told Beth she was a pretty useless bartender, so you know Mom, she gave him a piece of her mind, and Ferrus gave it right back to her, and I don't know what all, but Mom got so mad she took her Velveeta Cheesecake she was taking to the Wednesday bridge party over at Hagar Jump's, she took and slammed the cheesecake right into Ferrus's nasty old face, which is the only way he'll ever get any of her cheesecake.

"I don't know what happened after that, because I got a call from Miss Wanda over to the day-care to come and get the twins because they were fighting with Jason and Jeremy Goob, and then when I got home, you were in such a bad mood over the low price of crabs that I just stayed out of your way and here I am. I tell you, Huddie, I got through the whole day without fighting with anyone, and I intend to stay up here till things calm down, because it's safer up here."

Hudson takes a deep breath and one of his wife's cigarettes. "Believe I'll join you," he sighs, lying down to look up between the leaves at the stars.

A Modest Proposal at the Town Meeting

From the minutes of the last Oysterback Town Council Meeting:

OMAR HINTON: Okay, having got the Mosquito Festival Committee Report out of the way, the Chair recognizes Hudson Swann. Huddie has come up with a proposal that he thinks might solve the problem we've all been talking about, so let's give him a listen, folks. Huddie?

HUDSON SWANN: Thank you, Omar. And as president of the Fire Company, I'd like to thank all the folks on the Mosquito Festival Committee for their hard work. Since I'm not much of a public speaker unless I've got a bar counter and a beer, I'm gonna read this out loud from some index cards, and y'all will have to bear with me. The problem, as those who were here last week, or indeed anywhere in the West Hundred for the past two or three years, have noticed, is an invasion of human being foreigners on bicycles. Since there are ladies present, I won't use the word you hear most of the time to describe these types, but I don't think there's a person here who hasn't been plagued by this annoyance. We were thinking of appealing for help to the Gypsy Moth Control people, but it looks as if we're going to have to solve this one on our own.

Now, looking around here, I don't see anyone who has any particular objection to visitors coming around to enjoy what we have in Oysterback, as long as they're polite and clean up after themselves and don't scare the kids and the dogs, but this plague of foreigners from the Western Shore on these bicycles is getting out of control.

(Loud applause and cheers from the onlookers)

To begin with, these human beings don't seem to know the first thing about the rules of the road, and they just line up, five or six or fifty of 'em at a time, and weave all the hell over the road, blockin' up traffic and holdin' up progress while they comment on how quaint and cute we all are over here in rural America, without so much as a by-your-leave. And manners? Arrogant, rude, crude, and just plain *attitudinal* doesn't begin to describe it. Folks, we are talking your basic *obnoxious* here. Everybody's a tourist somewhere, but that doesn't mean you have to act like a pig at a two-for-one sale, or the Japanese in Shanghai. It seems to my good friend and colleague Junior Redmond and I that these human beings think the West Hundred is some kind of theme park called Watermanland, designed just for them by our beloved Governor Willie Don, and that we poor dumb locals are just here to add to the scenery while these Health Nazis breathe up our air, clog up our roadways, and comment loudly on our "primitive" lifestyle.

(*Hisses and jeers*)

Not only are these idiots, excuse me, human beings a danger to navigation on our highways and byways, they're a visual nuisance. Fellow citizens of Oysterback, I say your right to roll over my fifteen-year-old truck on a thousand-dollar bicycle and cram your ugly Western Shore behind into a pair of skin-tight lycra pants ends where my line of vision begins!

COUNCILPERSON GRINCH: Hear! Hear!

HUDSON SWANN: Therefore, after due study of the situation, the committee has come up with a solution that we feel will not only solve the problem of this dangerous annoyance in our midst, but also bring in some much-needed revenue to the town. What we have decided is that we ought to open a season on these bike-type human beings and issue gunning permits.

(*Loud applause*)

We figure we could sell 'em just like hunting licenses, and have the same rules as we do during deer season. Why, we could attract sportsmen from all over the Eastern Shore. What red-blooded Shoreman wouldn't be thrilled to have a two-hundred-pound accountant from Glen Burnie and a fifteen-speed Italian bike lashed to his bumper? With those stupid little helmets, bikers would make a wonderful trophy for your den or your TV room, up there next to your seventeen-point buck. Not only would this proposal thin out the dangerous menace these human beings create, it would also add considerable enjoyment to many who have been suffering through some hard times lately. And I guess that's about it. Thank you.

(*Mr. Swann sits down. Applause follows.*)

The resolution was passed by unanimous vote.

Letters to the *Oysterback Bugeye*

Dear Editor:

The Ladies of Oysterback Hardshell Methodist Church would like to thank all who made our recent Tater Tot Casserole Night such a big success. Plenty of money was raised for the new Recycling Center, which the town has decided to install right next to what used to be Widgeon Marsh until that big developer from Northern Virginia bought it and tried to turn it into Widgeon-on-Oysterback condos for foreigner yuppies from the Western Shore. Since everyone in town was there, there's no need to say that we're determined to make our organic waste composting station the biggest and best in the county.

Hagar (Mrs. Wimsey D.) Jump, Pres.

· · ·

Dear Helga,

I would appreciate it if you would let everyone know that Paisley Redmond has received his letter from the Blue Crab Tavern. Just because you are Junie Redmond's little brother and you have just come back from getting your A.A. degree in Auto Body Repair from some college in Detroit doesn't mean you have to go into the Blue Crab parking lot and make business for yourself on my brand new Monster Truck with a ball peen hammer.

Desiree Grinch, Prop.
Blue Crab Tavern

· · ·

Dear Editor:

Cancel my subscription to the *Bugeye*. I am outraged by your attitude concerning the Muskrat Skinning Contest. You women don't know anything about the subject and ought to stay home and cook, even if Desiree's girlfriend Doreen did win it this year, instead of the regular champion.

Name Withheld

Ed. note: Sour grapes, Johnny Ray Insley? I know your handwriting.

· · ·

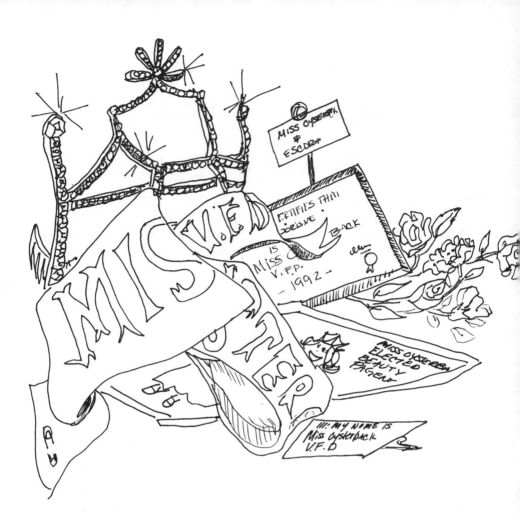

Dear Editor:

The family of Orville Tutweiler appreciates the many cards of sympathy and floral arrangements that were sent to Dreedle's Funeral Home. The floral arrangement of Orville's dog Elmer, done in brown and rust carnations, was particularly attractive.

Lee and Peggy Hinton Tutweiler

• • •

Dear Editor:

I am writing to tell you that when I gave you my secret recipe for chocolate velvet cake I accidentally put down one tablespoon of baking soda instead of one teaspoon. I hope this didn't cause too much trouble for anyone except I lost my glasses and can't see to write.

Mrs. Nettie M. Leery

Dear Editor:

I am writing to ask why the County can't patch that great big hole right in the middle of Red Toad Road where Hudson Swann and Junie Redmond had that accident with the dynamite caps over Easter. Where are our taxes going?

Ferrus T. Buckett

• • •

Dear Editor:

While we certainly appreciated your coverage of the birth of our new twin daughters, Amber Lee and Ashley Jennifer, we were sort of hoping that maybe the next time Jeanne goes into labor at the Curl Up 'n' Dye Salon de Beaute while she's cutting your hair, maybe you wouldn't interview her through the delivery?

Hudson Swann

Ed. note: For story and photos, see page 3.

• • •

Dear Editor:

For your information, that is my real hair and not a toupee as you suggested in your article "Money-Grubbing Mini-Trump Tries to Force Unwanted Condo Development on Town."

J. Snidely Grubb
Widgeon-on-Oysterback Condominiums
Wastedump, Va.

Ed. note: Oh right. And I am Queen Marie of Romania, bub.

• • •

Dear Editor:

I am really, really mad about that snobby Lisa Hackett winning the title of Miss Oysterback Volunteer Fire Department this year. I mean just because she is going with Second Lieutenant Teddy Paradise everyone thinks she's so special. Well, I want to tell you something! She pads! I saw it myself in the dressing room out behind where they usually keep the pumper. I think this is like totally unfair to those of us who used to go out with Teddy Paradise but now date Kevin Swann and don't need to pad. Thank you for listening to me. I know there will be an investigation.

Rikki Jane Insley

Ed. note: Chief Borrow promises to give this his full attention.

Girls' Night Out

Sometimes you get tired of your own cooking, as Miss Clara Barth of the McDaniel Country Store remarked when she came in here the other day for one of my new white potato pies.

I know what she means. Which is why Doreen Redmond, Jeanne Swann, and I—Desiree Grinch, proprietor of the Blue Crab Tavern— got into Doreen's red Cherokee the other night and drove down Route 13 to the Dew Drop Inn in Wingo, Virginia.

Usually, on girls' night out we go to Ocean City or somewhere there's a Kevin Costner movie. But that night Doreen had a craving for white potato pie, so it was the Dew Drop.

Now, I personally have nothing against the Dew Drop. The food is fine if you happen to like crackermeal crab cakes with one sliver of claw meat swimming in a vat of grease, and you like to drink with the terminally common sorry. If Litey Clash had to use his own ladies' room, he might clean it once in a while, but that is just my opinion.

I should have known there would be trouble the minute I saw Snake Wingate's truck in the lot. Snake, as we all know, is real fractious. But Doreen wanted that white potato pie, and by then Jeanne had to go to the bathroom, so we went in and took a booth.

I took one look around and I knew there was trouble even before Litey Clash came shuffling up to us without, for once, that big stretched-out smile all over his face.

Eyeball to eyeball, Snake was holding onto a longneck bottle by the wrong end, and that lawyer was about to bean him with his brief case, and everyone else was getting out of the way.

"Desiree," Litey says, "in the ordinary course of events, you know that I would be more than happy to have you and these fine Oyster-backettes boil the dishrag in my place, but it looks as if there is going to be trouble and I think you ought to leave before it starts.

"That there lawyer represented Logene, who is, as you know, the ex-Mrs. Snake, in the divorce, and as he and Snake were both on their way in here, Logene sped past, stopped and tried to run one of them down in the parking lot, and now each of them says she was aiming for him, not the other one."

If you ask me, that's why Litey has the sheriff in his place all the time; he doesn't know how to handle people.

"Let me take care of this," I said, and went over to Snake and this lawyer, who were about a breath away from feathering up on each other. It was right tense.

"Before you two start a who-shot-John," I said, getting right in between them, "I believe I can settle this argument. Will you agree to wait for one minute while I step outside and inspect the scene of the incident?"

Snake looked at the lawyer, and the lawyer looked at Snake, and they both nodded. "We'll let Ms. Grinch make the call," agrees the lawyer.

It took me about thirty seconds to go outside and check the parking lot, and when I came back I knew the answer.

"Well?" says Snake. "Who was she about to hit and run, Desiree? Me or this common sorry courthouse barnacle?"

"Well," I said, "There were two sets of tire marks, like she tried once, backed up, and tried again. Is that right?"

They both nodded.

"Well, then I am here to tell you when big court convenes, Logene, formerly Mrs. Snake, tried to run down this here lawyer," I said firmly.

"How you figure that?" Snake asked. He's a good enough pitcher, but you have to spell it all out for him off the field.

"Well, it's like this," I told them. "The difference is between runnin' down a snake and runnin' down a lawyer. You don't back up and try to hit the snake twice."

Anyway, that's how I come away with Litey Clash's white potato pie recipe. Hope you like it.

Quite Quaint They Ain't

Everyone has got to be a tourist somewhere. At least that is what I, Desiree Grinch, proprietor of the Blue Crab Tavern, believe, and I have been a tourist in enough places to know that of which I speak.

Still and all, after that unfortunate incident with the late, unlamented Haney Sparks at the Mosquito Festival a couple of years ago, we don't get the tour buses anymore, which is just as well, all things considered. They tended to be filled up with little old ladies with blue hair who are all looking to spend their widow's mite looking for husband number two, and it was driving Ferrus T. Buckett crazy, as he is the town's only eligible senior-citizen bachelor, and he gets irritated like you could not believe. Ferrus isn't a misogynist or a bigot, mind; he doesn't like *anybody*.

I guess that's why we were all surprised when these two little old ladies with blue hair and a copy of something like Ye Olde Guide to Ye Quainte Eastern Shore wandered into the Blue Crab the other night. "We're here," one of them says to me, just as cute as a little red wagon, "to see all the quaint Eastern Shore characters Mr. Michener talks about in *Chesapeake*."

I was brought up to have respect for little old ladies, and heaven knows, I plan to be one myself someday, but I had to hold my tongue between you and me, if I had a nickel for every time I've heard some Shoreperson curse that book for bringing all these tourists and transplant foreigners in here, I would not be running this place; I would be in the Caribbean with Harrison Ford, sipping mai-tais on the beach, thank you very much.

But they were so sweet, and so nice, and asked for double gin screwdrivers and keep them coming, that I said, "Well, if it is Eastern Shore characters you want to see, you have come to the right place, for this is Friday night and every waterman, every skipjack captain and crew will be in here tonight, and you will certainly have your full share of local color. In Oysterback, as my friend Captain Saloman says, we have characters we haven't even used yet."

That pleased them so much they took a table within earfall of the bar and ordered Oysters Desiree ($12.95 entree price), which of course pleased me no end.

"Ferrus," I hissed as I went on by him, "you be nice to those two blue-haired ladies. Or at least, don't try to cadge drinks off them." Ferrus just snorted into his rock 'n' rye and started to recite some of his poetry. Except it's really Robert Service's.

Long about then, Hudson Swann and Junior Redmond come in, still in their gumboots.

I could tell they had come from the program because Huddie says, sort of mulling it over, "I never knew Reinhold Niebuhr wrote the Serenity Prayer. He must be spinning in his grave every time someone else stamps that prayer on a piece of varnished cedar with a decal of the Last Supper."

"And he's not gettin' any royalties, either," Junie added indignantly. "Say, there, gimme one a them designer waters, Des, that's a friend."

I opened his lime-flavored Perrier and slid it down the bar.

"Is the espresso machine working?" Huddie asked. "I'm cold to the bone. Wind's up and down the mast today."

"Russell Means, Best Supporting Actor, *Last of the Mohicans*. Hollywood loves Native Americans," Ferrus growled, just loud enough for everyone to hear it. From time to time, as everyone knows, he predicts the Oscars. It's a God-given talent.

Just about then, Deputy Sheriff Johnny Ray Insley came running in, all out of breath. "Everybody come! Aliens from Uranus are trying to break into the seafood plant over to Patamoke! We need all the help we can get!"

"Hot damn!" Junie yells, coming alive. "Come on, Huddie, they need us!"

"Sounds awful-like!" Huddie says. The two of them picked up Ferrus and scrambled out of the bar like I'd reminded them about their tab. There was a roar of pickup trucks in the parking lot, and the siren faded into the distance. The sudden silence was deafening. You could actually hear the juke box.

Life may not be the same since those two started doing the twelve-step dance, but it hasn't slowed down any, either.

"It isn't all like Mr. Michener wrote," one of the little old ladies said. I don't think she was disappointed.

A Voice from the Past

"What do you think of those glads?" Miss Nettie asks her married daughter, Jeanne Swann. Miss Nettie reaches out and pulls the stem of red flowers toward her, the blossoms passing through her gentle fingers. "These are crimson hearts; they're an old, old variety, you know. I dug up some bulbs from a corner of the old schoolhouse two falls ago; they were all overgrown with honeysuckle over there." She releases the stalk, and it springs back, ruffled blossoms trembling up to the sunlight.

"Here, in this corner of the garden they get enough sun, and the color sets off the orange and pink in the zinnias, just as they're starting to bloom."

She whips out her secateurs, pruning the withered head off a branch of love-in-a-mist, which she stuffs into the pocket of her apron. "If I could paint a picture, like Larrimore Briscoe, I'd paint this garden in late summer," she sighs.

"I can never see these old flowers without thinking about family and old friends. This love-in-a-mist, now, it came from one that my grandmother put in by her back porch when I was first married. I can remember now how we used to sit there on hot summer nights, singing. Your great aunt Miriam played the guitar, and we'd sing all the popular songs, boys and girls together. "Mockingbird Hill," "The Tennessee Waltz." The boys used to come by boat, those nights, from Elliot's Island and over to Wallopsville. We used to go to Patamoke to the dances they had there then, in those days after the war."

Her voice is soft and thoughtful. In the long evening light, she almost looks young again. "That's where I first met your father, you know, over to those dances at Patamoke. I was nineteen then, and working for the phone company. I had my little black Ford coupe, and I thought I was very sophisticated. He'd come back from the war, you know, and was working on his father's farm, going to school at night, on the G.I. Bill. I was wearing a yellow dress, and Mariam was wearing blue, and I saw him come in with my brother, and I said, 'That's the man for me.' Alva Leery. What a funny name, Alva, I thought, but it didn't stop me for a minute. Your father was a very handsome man when he was younger."

A yellow rambler has taken over the back fence, full of big, blooming cabbage roses the color of fresh buttercream. "We planted this the year we moved into this house," Miss Nettie says. "I stole the cutting from the dance hall down to Patamoke. Don't look at me like that. Didn't you know that cuttings won't thrive unless you 'steal' them? Oh, your father used to tease me about my flowers, but he loved to look at them. You know, someone asked me the other day, if you could have someone back from the dead for ten minutes, alive all over again, would you wish it?"

Snip, and she hands Jeanne a branch of roses. "I thought about your father, and finally, I thought, no. Listen; *it's hard enough to lose people one time, let alone to have them back only to lose them again.* The past is a nice place to visit, but you don't want to live there. You have to cherish what you have here and now, do the best you can for the future. If he says he's willing to meet you halfway, then you meet him halfway."

Miss Nettie smiles, and there is a glimpse of the ghost of the girl who drove that Ford coupe and worked for the phone company in her face. Snip with the secateurs, and the withered head of a rose falls to the ground.

"Men," she pronounces, "are like little puppies, and you have to treat them that way. They never grow up. But then, neither do we. I'm a mother and a grandmother and I still don't feel like a grownup."

Miss Nettie's secaturs snip. "We've all got to meet each other halfway," she sighs.

This Just in from the *Bugeye*

THE BIG EXCITEMENT last week was the Oysterback High School Reunion, held at the old Oysterback High School. The Boone Brothers, Mike and Gabe, Class of '68, showed up, surprising many people, since they have not been seen since 1969. Asked where they'd been and what they'd been doing all these years, Mike Boone said they'd been living off the land, over to Uranus. Finding out the Vietnam war was over in 1975, they decided they might stick around and open a fix-it shop over to Tubman's Corners where the old gas station used to be. Gabe says if you can remember the sixties, you probably weren't there.

• • •

STATE DELEGATE ORVILLE ORVALL, Class of '71, out on bail, also showed up for the class reunion. He says the charges were put up by Iranian terrorists, and he expects to be vindicated in next month's hearing. Once again, someone asked this editor why we kept returning Orville to Annapolis, term after term. Orville's brief visit was a reminder to all about why we want to keep him as far away from us as possible. Chief Briscoe says charges will be pressed concerning the damage to the ATM and the lobbyists. Charlene Tutweiler, Miss Devanaux County Poultry Industry, is filing a separate suit in Circuit Court.

• • •

OVER TO OMAR HINTON'S STORE, Faraday Hicks, Oysterback's only fully licensed vegetarian, had a massive coronary the other day. His pacemaker seized up in front of the microwave while he was heating up a nacho and olive loaf sandwich. His wife, Thelma, tells us he's resting comfortably. Get well soon, Faraday! And incidentally, Omar wants everyone to know that the new ice cream flavor, Tuna Fudge Twirl, is now in stock.

• • •

THE COUNTRY JAZZ SOUNDS of Bird Dog and the Road Kings will be heard at the wedding reception of Carter "Pork" Ebling and Crystal Tiffany Tutweiler this Saturday at the Wallopsville Fire Hall. Stag and drag, coats and ties for all the guys. For times and tickets, call Tiffany's

mom, Gladys, at Bob's Gas 'n' Go. Omar Hinton wants everyone to know Tiffany's pattern is registered with Hinton's Store in Oysterback.

• • •

COL. BOB "MAD DOG" TUTWEILER wants everyone to know that was not him last week on *America's Most Wanted* but his evil twin Sonny who was last seen somewhere in California, where you can expect that kind of behavior from people.

• • •

REVEREND CLAUDE CROUCH, the Traveling Evangelist, struck his tent last week and moved on to Virginia Beach after receiving a sign from God that True Doctrine commanded him to open a transmission repair business. He says he will be shifting gears for God on the sawdust trail.

• • •

IF YOU SEE HUDSON SWANN'S pickup truck rolling around town without anyone seeming to be at the wheel, relax. Seems Huddie has been teaching his twins to drive. Since they're not big enough yet to reach the pedals, Amber works the gas, the brake, and the clutch while Ashley steers and shifts, and vice versa. Hudson says they're better drivers than most adults, but he still won't let them drive anywhere but up and down Razor Strap Road without him.

• • •

THE PATAMOKE DESIGNER HOUSE, to benefit Patamoke Community Theatre in the Oblong, will open next week. The theme is "Country Style," and over six noted local decorators have been invited to design rooms in the old Gersen place, where that terrible murder happened about fifteen years ago. It has been rumored to be haunted ever since, since no one ever stays there very long. Most people will know it as the Jaycee's Hallowe'en Haunted House. Of particular interest, we understand, is Letty's Buttons 'n' Bows, Inc. room, done in a bendover theme, featuring the country crafts of Oysterback's very own Parsons Dreedle, who wants everyone to know that he has added lawn ornaments to the line of homegrown produce he sells in front of Dreedle's Funeral Home.

• • •

OVER TO WALLOPSVILLE, Hurley Whortley and Misti Clash have celebrated their engagement by going to Elkton for matching tattoos. They plan to marry in June, shortly after Donnie, their youngest, graduates from high school. "We would have done it before, but the kids were all against it," Misti reports.

• • •

THERE WAS A STIR when the Civil War re-enactors who were camped out down by Widgeon Marsh last week to celebrate the anniversary of the Skirmish of Swann's Farm reported sightings of unidentified flying objects. After everyone had calmed down a little, Chief Briscoe fingered the UFO aliens as some of Widgeon Marsh's smaller mosquitoes.

The Devil, Steve Meachum, and All Their Works

G host is the term a lot of old watermen use for abandoned work-
boats towed up a gut or down some creek and left to the mercy of
the elements.

Such a boat has already long outlived its usefulness, full of rot and
worms, for watermen are a handy lot who will repair and make do with
a beloved boat until she's all rope, patch, and jury rig, even leave her up
on the stands in the back yard, stripping her for parts, before taking her
on that last journey up the gut or down the marsh.

Yet the *Mary Jane* lies under about six feet of water at the head of a
deep creek, almost as intact as the day she came off the stands at Bainey
Mills' boatyard, not even two hundred miles on her corroding marine
engine, not even a second season's paint on her hogged hull.

And she has lain there some time, long enough for the oil to seep out of
her engine house in a rainbow puddle on the water's surface, for the soft
river mud to coat her with a fine green blanket as she settles into that
viscous embrace, rotting by inches on the turn of the moon and the tides.

No crab will crawl into that watery cabin to shed, and no schools of
silver minnows seek refuge from the snappers in her bloated washboards. No living thing will come near her as she lies like a corpse at the
bottom of the creekhead, waiting for Resurrection Day. You can still see
the color, just beneath the still waters in that quiet cove where no one
goes.

The odd thing is, she is painted blood red.

Here's the story.

Steve Meachum was born bad. Steve Meachum was a thief, a liar, a
bully, and worse. Most people, at least people who were smaller and
weaker than he, gave him a wide berth. He was bad to the bone. No
socially redeeming value. So bad that even the working girls who cruise
the strip on Kent Island stayed away from him. A guy from Northeast
who was in 'Nam with him said that he'd never seen a man who took so
much pleasure in killing, and he did not say this in a joking way.

Lots of people down to the harbor had often heard him say he wished
he had a boat like the *Mary Jane*. Some other people said that he'd been

crabbing nearby in his rotten old boat when the boy who had her built went overboard and drowned. Some people said that Steve Meachum could have helped that boy, but he didn't. Some other people said that he helped that boy drown, holding him down with a crab net while the kid struggled for the surface. What Steve did was buy up the *Mary Jane* from the boy's wife for about a third of what she was worth.

He painted her red from bow to stern. Now everyone knows that a man who's painted his workboat red has seen the devil, that's common knowledge. That someone who paints his boat red is trying to make a basic statement about his badness is common sense. Also, every sailor knows that red is the hardest color to see on the open water, so it was easy to figure out that Steve Meachum was up to nothing good, stealing crab pots, tools, gas, live boxes, and everything else that wasn't nailed down or locked up.

It was just that no one could ever catch him at it, though everyone had their suspicions, although just like the boy who drowned, no one could prove anything.

"Steve," a boy from Saxis called to him on the radio one day, just fooling around, "I see you've got your boat painted red. You see the devil?"

"I *am* the devil," Steve replied, laughing that hollow, unfunny laugh of his. And he believed it, too. He thought he was bad, you understand. Like most people who think they're bad, he just wasn't bad enough.

With that bit of arrogance, Steve tempted fate once too often, for that night he went to the back room of the bar to play cards, and no one was there but this one stranger. This stranger was a weird-looking dude, with a misshapen hat pulled low over his ears, and a dark fire in his eyes, like smoldering ash. When he smiled, his teeth were pointed, as if he'd filed them down, and they glittered in the neon light. "Play some cards, bunk?" he asked, and his voice was like the hiss of water on hot coals.

"I'll deal," Steve said, sitting down and reaching for the deck.

Now, there's a waterman's card game called tonk, which is a lot like gin, only different, and that's what Steve and the stranger sat down to play. Even at his cheating best, Steve was losing hand after hand, and pretty soon he was down to nothing. "You'll have to take my IOU," he said, and the stranger just smiled, showing all those pointy teeth.

"I know better than to take your marker," the stranger said. He shuffled the cards through his long fingers, and cut them, once, twice, three times, face down on the table.

"We'll play this hand for the *Mary Jane,*" he said. And then, looking at Steve from beneath his hat, he added in his hissing voice, "That is, if you're not too chicken."

Like a lot of bullies, Steve was a chicken, but he was also full of Heaven Hell and methadrine, and he just sneered. "Deal," he said. There were beads of sweat on his upper lip.

He laid down forty-five, and the stranger laid down sixty. Before Steve could protest, the stranger swept the cards up off the table; a stray card fell from the sleeve of his shirt, fluttering to the floor.

"Damn you!" Steve cried, falling under the table to scrabble for the card in the peanut shells on the floor. It was then that he saw the stranger's feet.

They were like the hoofs of a goat, and Steve Meachum suddenly knew who he was playing with, and it was no mortal man, but the Devil himself.

"Oh, Lord," Steve Meachum said, but it was too late. Slowly, the face of the Devil dropped beneath the table until he was grinning eyeball to eyeball with the waterman.

"So you say you're the Devil," Old Scratch said, vastly amused. His bony hand gripped Steve's arm. "Well, then, bunk, you'll come off to Hell with me!"

At least that's what they say happened to Steve Meachum. No one saw him again, at least not in this world. All that was left in the back room was a deck of cards scattered all over the floor and the table, and the faint smell of sulphur in the air. One thing is sure, no one's seen Steve Meachum since that night.

Shortly after, someone, maybe a few someones, towed the *Mary Jane* up the creek and scuttled her there. And there she lies, until she rots or the Devil claims his winnings, whichever comes first.

At least that's what they say.

Angels Unawares

All day, the skies had been the fishbelly white that comes before snow. Dense white flakes the size of saucers had begun to fall when Doreen Redmond wheeled her cart out to the Buy and Bag parking lot. She glanced at her watch and muttered. Doreen was one of those people who are constitutionally unable to go into town without running into at least five people they know, and stopping to talk to three of them at length. As she piled her groceries into the back of the Cherokee, she decided she would be home by the time the kids got out of school if she took Marsh Road.

"Through the Haunted Marsh," she told herself. There was just something about that desolate causeway that made you feel as if you'd dropped off the planet, made you want to put the pedal to the metal and barrel on through those four or five winding miles of endless, barren marsh until you reached Tubman's Corners. No redwing blackbirds ever sang there, no marshmallows ever bloomed. Not so much as a tide seemed to flow through Haunted Marsh. Even the trappers avoided it; nothing seemed to live there but an endless sea of bile-yellow grass. It was eerie, she always thought; most wetlands are teeming places, cities of wildlife.

The snow flew at Doreen's windshield, all but blinding her. She squinted to see the road in the gathering dusk of early winter, but all she could see was blowing snowflakes. When the mangy doe burst from the snow and hurtled across the causeway, her first thought was that something evil was chasing it. Automatically, she slammed on the brakes and turned the wheel sharply. Bad move, she thought, even as she was doing it.

In slow motion, she slid across the icy asphalt. Gallon jugs of milk, boxes of cereal careened from the grocery bags. The Jeep rolled into the grass, sinking in the soft mud. She cursed, shifted into four-wheel drive, tried to back out to the asphalt again, but the wheels spun deeper and deeper into the muck.

"Hell ain't half full," she sighed. A woman of few fears, she still hesitated before opening the door and climbing down to survey the damage. It wasn't good, she thought, looking at the front wheels sunk a foot deep into the slushy mud. In the seconds it took for her to walk around the shoulder, snow stuck to her hair, and she was almost blinded by the white wind.

So preoccupied was she with her next move that she did not see the truck looming out of the darkness until it was almost upon her. And even then, it was the rocking bang of its ancient engine that caught her attention; the headlights barely penetrated the gale.

Doreen Redmond had seen some old pickup trucks in her time, but this one could have qualified for historical plates. Beneath layers of mud, dust, and rust, it was held together with bailing wire and duct tape; steam rose from the hood. Slowly, the passenger window creaked down and a face that was all beard, hair, and John Deere cap peered out at her. "You need help." It was a statement of fact, not a question.

From the driver's window, another face, all beard and bandanna, appeared. "We got a log chain in the back."

She watched as two rawboned men in antique coveralls climbed down from the ancient truck and inspected her rear axle. They smelled like kerosene, manure, and old sweat overlaid with the pungent aroma of home-grown and home-brewed. Flying snow stuck to their flying hair.

"We kin fix 'is," the driver said, showing missing teeth as he walked past her in the swirling white beam of her headlights. "We're the Boone Brothers. We fix just about any damn thing that's gone up." There it was on the side of the truck, beneath the crust, hand-painted in careful block letters:

BOONE BROS
WE FIX

Without another word, they went to work with the log chain and the pick. In five minutes, the Cherokee was back on the causeway again, headed for Oysterback. Doreen reached for her purse, grappled for the proper words of thanks. She was speechless, something new for a woman of many words. "Thank you," she said over and over again.

"It weren't nothin'," said the driving Boone as he removed a pint bottle from his pocket and took a healthy swig. His hands were encrusted with black grime. He offered it to Doreen, who shook her head and babbled gratefully about payment, free haircuts from the Salon de Beaute, a bushel of oysters, groceries, whatever, anything.

"Don't need none a that. We live off the land," the other Boone Brother said, taking the pint. After a last inspection of the Cherokee, the Boone Brothers climbed back into their truck. Doreen gratefully sank into the warmth of her cab. As the ancient truck lumbered up alongside the Cherokee, the passenger window opened and a Boone Brother thrust his hirsute head out the window. The sound of "Dark Side of the Moon" and the smell of killer weed spilled out of the cab into the snowy twilight.

"Y'know, lady," the Boone Brother said earnestly, "Ya really oughta be careful. There's all *kindsa* weird people out here these days."

Last Call

I f you're looking for someone with whom to ponder the imponderable, you'd better look elsewhere. I, Desiree Grinch, Proprietor of the Blue Crab Tavern, have not had a metaphysical thought since I dropped out of college and gave up black tights.

Which is why I was surprised when, real late the other night, I looked up and saw the ghost of Haney Sparks walk into the Blue Crab.

I knew it was Haney Sparks's ghost because, for one thing, he was dressed like he had been hitting John Travolta's yard sales, and for another you could sort of see through him.

I, Desiree Grinch, am not afraid of ghosts like some people I know. If you can survive one of those Jello Mold Suppers down to the Fire Hall, then nothing else will ever scare you again.

Well, Haney pulled up a barstool and sat down, or rather, he sort of drifted across the seat.

"I'd like a draft," he says, very polite. So I pulled him a draft. All the sign over the bar says is that we do not serve unpleasant people, nothing about dead ones. Since Haney had been unpleasant in life, however, I reserved the right to toss him out should he start up in death.

He sort of sat there and inhaled the beer, which he obviously could not drink, since his hand went through the mug every time he tried to pick it up.

"I always thought souls in Hell cried out for ice water, not Bud Lite," I remarked. Like I said before, Haney had not been the most pleasant person in Oysterback when he was alive.

He settled his features into a real hurt look. "It took me a long time to get here," he said. "The least you could do is be polite to me. Jeez, Des, you would not believe what Hell is like."

"I do not smell any sulphur or brimstone on you." I said. "Therefore I assume you will tell me that Hell is not as I have always pictured it."

Haney looked longingly at a slice of black walnut pie on the counter. I gave it to him, and he sniffed at it. When he was done, he sort of sighed. "In Hell, there's cable TV, but there's never anything on but reruns of *McHale's Navy* dubbed into Uhuru, which I do not understand a word of. And the food is terrible—tuna noodle casserole with Tater Tot toppings."

I shuddered in spite of myself. For a man who enjoyed his TV and food as much as the late Haney, this was indeed a punishing eternity. I cut him a slice of my orange meringue pie and watched him sort of sniggle up the essence of it.

"And everyone has to wear polyester/acrylic-blend Da-Glo lime green leisure suits." He leaned so close to me that I could smell the graveyard on his breath. "The Devil wears white patent leather shoes and a matching belt with his," Haney whispered.

"Ugh," said I, who never let an unnatural fiber touch my body. I served him a couple of my chocolate logs, I felt that bad. He enjoyed them as best he could, snorting and sniffing.

"But the worse thing, Des, is the decor. It's like a big, not-too-clean, bus-station restroom that always smells like vomit and cheap disinfectant. And, and," he choked, a ghostly, ghastly sound, as he tried to wrap his cold fingers around my wrist for emphasis, "you're always in there, waiting for a bus that *never comes!*"

It took all I had not to scream in terror.

Just then the clock over the pool table struck midnight.

"That's last call," Haney sobbed. "I got to git my bill and pay up and get back." He reached into his pocket and brought out his spectral wallet. Of course, they have money in Hell.

As I gave him his change, I said, "I don't get many ghosts in here."

Haney looked at the coins in his hand. Before he could leave me a tip, he started to fade away, his voice getting faint.

"And at these prices, you're not likely to get any more, either."

Hell's too good for Haney Sparks, if you ask me.

Where They Take Christmas Seriously

Dear Misha,

I really loved your last letter about the benefit for Rob MacQuay and all the doings in the Business. I do miss the life and my friends. There's no way I could have known, when I was playing Nellie Forbush at the Patamoke Dinner Theatre in the Oblong last summer, that I would end up married to the cute fireman who came about the grease fire in the dressing rooms. But I doubt that even Toby could find a role for a nine-months pregnant actress.

Besides, with Paisley oystering in Rock Hall and little Olivier still due any second now, it's less lonely over here with his family, especially at Christmas. And it seems to me that they take Christmas real seriously over here. Maybe it's because I am not related to everyone within a ten-mile radius, or maybe it's because I never had a family before, but believe me, Christmas in Oysterback is something else.

To begin with, Mr. Eddie, the new hairdresser at the Curl Up 'n' Dye Salon de Beaute, has inaugurated community theater in the West Hundred and cast me as the Virgin Mary in the Living Christmas Pageant. I think he was sort of hoping for a two-for-one deal, but no such luck. Hudson Swann, Junior Redmond, and Earl Don Grinch played the Three Wise Men, and Mr. Eddie was quite put out when they showed up in full VFD regalia and announced to little June Debbie Redmond's Baby Oh-Oh doll in the manger that they had "come from a fahr." The good ole boys love to make fun of Mr. Eddie, I guess.

I am still waitressing for Desiree Grinch at the Blue Crab. She says when Olivier does come, we will just put him or her into the big sty-rofoam cooler and keep on going. I think she is serious about this, although she has been bahing and humbugging a lot. Her theme for the Blue Crab this year is "An Elvis Christmas." She put all the King's Christmas albums on the juke and strung blue lights up over the pool table and the bar.

Desiree says she understands the demands of the Business since she used to be an exotic dancer on the Block when she was married to her second husband, Mario Mildeaux, up there. She has been letting me

emcee Open Mike Night at the Blue Crab, and it was quite touching to hear Ferrus T. Buckett sing "Silent Night" accompanied by his dog Blackie.

Captain Hardee Swann again blew out all the power in Oysterback when he turned on his Christmas decorations. Hudson says his father has got to get a new retirement hobby, as this one is driving his mom, Miss Catherine, crazy.

Captain Hardee had to get Earl Don over to their house with the power company's cherry picker to help him install the light-up Santa in the chimney, the sleigh and nine reindeer and Santa that he put on the ridgepole, the star on the TV antenna, the six choirboys on the roof, flanked by candy canes, the carolers on the front porch, two sets of five each, about nine candles scattered all over the yard, three Frosty the Snowmen, and the complete nine-figure Nativity scene down by the crepe myrtle bushes. He has about four miles of string lights, too, and he not only outlined the whole house, but also the garage and the 1956 Chevy pickup that's been rusting out down by the dock for years. All the hibiscus bushes blink on and off from Thanksgiving to New Year's. Omar Hinton is furious about all the ice cream melting in the freezer at his store, but Miss Catherine says Captain Hardee never drank or chased women, and the kids come from miles around to see the house, so it's something.

Dinner is at Miss Nettie Leery's. My arteries get clogged with sweet potato and marshmallow roll, oyster fritters, cornbread with bacon, creamed spinach, creamed corn, creamed squash, mushroom soup and stringbean casserole, cranberry surprise, and my fair share of a turkey the size of a Volkswagen. I could only groan when Miss Nettie asked if I wanted any of the jello mold, but I did manage to find room for a piece of Mr. Eddie's pecan pumpkin rum chiffon pie. Mr. Eddie told Desiree and me that he wants to write a cookbook called "Homo on the Range." No one else would get it, he said, but us. But they all ate the pie, every last crumb.

Just as Reverend Briscoe was about to pronounce the halftime Christmas blessing, the phone rang. It was Paisley. He'd finally gotten through from Rock Hall, and I just took the phone out on the front porch and we had a lovely husband and wife talk without the whole family wanting to get on the line.

I guess Captain Hardee went off at halftime and plugged in his Christmas lights, because for one beautiful moment, the Swann home-place and all of Oysterback lit up like Broadway. Then the whole town went black. I tried to tell Paisley about it all, but he said he already knew, and next year he, I, and Olivier were having a Baltimore actor Christmas. I guess he's not impressed. But he was laughing.

But in the dark and stillness, you could hear Ferrus T. Buckett singing "Silent Night" with Blackie.

As I say, Christmas is serious in Oysterback. Tell everyone I miss them. Write soon.

Love, Beth

Make a Joyful Noise

As hard is it is for some people to believe, I was churched as a child, and somewhere or other I have the gold Sunday school stars to prove it. So, if I, Desiree Grinch, proprietor of the Blue Crab Tavern, am a heathen, it's certainly not my parents' fault.

There's something real interesting in the fact that religion is one of those deeply personal and private matters that people seem to enjoy murdering, swindling, torturing, and raping over, isn't there? (You know who you are, and *shame* on you, too.)

But one Sunday every year, I head down the road to Wittman, to the New St. John's Methodist Church, to attend the Gospel Song Feast. You see, once a year, Reverend Ella Everett comes over from Baltimore with two busloads of folks from the Former Rose of Sharon Baptist Church, and I wouldn't miss that for the worldly world. I call Reverend Everett *Mother,* and so do a lot of other people you might not think of in those terms. The purity of that woman's heart just shines out of her. She's up in years now and in a chair, but that doesn't stop her from being one of the most spiritual people I've ever met in my life.

You can take all your Orals and your Tammy Fayes and your Maharishis and sew 'em up in a sack as far as I am concerned; I'll take Mother any day. When you meet a genuinely holy person, you know it. They freely *give* spiritual comfort and advice; they *don't* ask for a Mercedes or their very own theme park in Florida. Mother's a saintly woman whose faith is real, whose blessing I'm humbled to ask for and receive. She can look right into your soul and tell you things no one else knows, see right down into the places where your secrets live. Now, that's a gift.

Pagan, I might be, but I hope that I'm not so cynical that I don't know sincerity and faith when I see it in someone else. Besides, Reverend Everett is a Shorewoman who was raised right down the road in Claiborne, who picked berries to put herself through school, who knows adversity, endurance, and belief. When there's a Gospel Song Feast, there's food for the soul and food for the body, and there's the music.

Now you may say, what does this white woman know about African-

American church music, and all I can say is I know what I like, and it's
not a soloist standing under a baby spot with a microphone, crooning
some syrupy slush like a Las Vegas lounge singer, as I have seen, and
some people like that and that is their right.

What I want is Reverend Joyce Jenkins singing "Precious Lord."
Now, I am here to tell you, that woman has the gift. When that molten
gold voice tells you "His Eye is on the Sparrow," it's enough to make an
atheist believe. That woman's mezzo can fill up a church to the rafters
and touch you where you live. And you haven't lived until you've heard
her handle "God Will Take Care of You."

Then there's Sister Margaret Johnson, with a contralto that must
wake up Bessie Smith, rich and deep and from the heart. And there's the
Rose of Sharon Inspirational Singers and Sister Patricia Brown and
Friends. *That's* church music. That's the place in the heart from which
Aretha and Otis came. It's the music of George Jones and Kitty Wells.
It's not just African-American music, it's not just white music; it's the
source of all that is uniquely American in our culture, and it belongs to
all of us. Come the holidays, I want the Five Blind Boys singing "White
Christmas," not the Chipmunks.

Besides, if gospel was good enough for Elvis, it ought to be good
enough for you.

Philo Redux

It was about the time that Jeanne took the twins and ran off to Ocean City with Mr. Eddie, the new hairdresser down at the Salon de Beaute, that Hudson Swann took to drinking pretty hard. I guess Mr. Eddie wasn't as gay as we all thought.

A couple of times, I, Desiree Grinch, proprietor of the Blue Crab Tavern here in Oysterback, had to have my ex, Earl Don, drive him home. It's a sorry thing to see a man walking around with a look on his face as if the rug beneath his whole world has been pulled out from beneath him; he and Jeanne were high-school sweethearts, and he just lived for those twin girls, Ashley and Amber.

Not that I don't understand just how Jeanne Swann must have felt; it's a hard thing when your marriage is reduced to the lyrics of a particularly sappy country-and-western song, which is why Earl Don is my ex and not my present. This way, he has to stay on his toes and keep the fires burning. I guess Mr. Eddie knows how to light a match.

All Huddie had left was his dog, Philo. Jeanne never did take much to that black Lab, or I guess she would have taken him to Ocean City with her when she and Mr. Eddie left. Philo is not an easy dog to like. First of all, he's about as dumb as . . . well, let me put it the way my Aunt Walhalla would have said: If that dog's brains were put on a fork, it would look like a BB rolling down a four-lane highway.

When Philo wasn't riding around in the workboat with Huddie, or hanging out of the back of a pickup truck with his tongue flying in the wind, he was out in back of the yard, lying under the crepe myrtle on his back, all four legs going at once, as if he was running in his dreams. I hate to say a bad thing about a poor creature that can't fight back, but Philo was about the most useless dog there ever was.

He couldn't hunt, because he was gun-shy and just as like to crawl up your leg when he heard a shotgun as go after a bird. And he got seasick all over the boat, too, even though he insisted on going out. Spoiled a fishing trip for us one time when he ate all the peelers.

That's the way Philo was, but Hudson had had him since he was a puppy, and he was as attached to that dog as Hudson was to his own

daughters. Philo would follow him anywhere, and if he went off, the poor dumb dog would sit at the end of the dock or the drive and wait until he came back.

Junie Redmond has been Hudson's best friend since they were put in the same crib together, and even he couldn't stand Philo around him too much because Philo always smelled like wet dog, even during last summer's drought. When Jeanne walked out on Hudson, Junior suggested that a part of the reason might have been that Mr. Eddie didn't have a smelly dumb dog that didn't have enough sense not to eat rotten crabs and lie under the crepe myrtle.

I personally am very fond of dogs, but I do not wish to have them in the Blue Crab, as this is liable to upset the health inspectors. So Philo had to sit outside in the pickup truck whenever Hudson was in the Blue Crab, which was entirely too much right after Jeanne left him.

Now I think that there are times when a person has a right to get drunk and stay drunk, as long as the person does not drive, or drive anyone crazy, or get mean and trash my Elvis poster. Hudson did none of these things; he merely sat in a corner of the bar nursing shots of Heaven Hell. If he had asked me my advice, I would have given it to him, which is that he should think less about running around with the boys and worrying about his truck, his boat, and his hunting and fishing, and more about pleasing his wife, but no one asked me, so I kept my thoughts to myself. But if you want my opinion, men who can only express their feelings in about sixty words, half of which refer to moving engine parts, are in serious trouble when it comes to pleasing women.

Even so, I hate to see a man play "You've Lost That Lovin' Feelin'" 389 times straight on my juke box. It is bad for business and worse for my morale, especially at this time of year when most watermen are thinking about eeling and making their workboat payments, not spending the day in a bar.

So, I guess in a way it was Hudson's own fault when Philo finally got tired of waiting for him and took off, too.

At first, Huddie thought Philo had gone after a lady dog, since one of Ferrus's bitches is in heat and it is spring. After a while, he stirred himself enough to put up some signs around the neighborhood and, finally, an ad in the paper. Still, a week went by and no Philo. No wife, no kids, and no dog. It was a sad thing.

Hudson was just about heartbroken. I didn't think he could get any sadder. Beth Redmond, my barmaid, had taken to sweeping the floor around him and giving him a flick with the feather duster, he'd become that much a part of the decor at the Blue Crab.

Then one day last week, when he was sitting in the corner drinking Heaven Hell and looking for quarters to put in the juke box, who should walk in but Jeanne.

Well, she says, I am back and I hope you are ready to talk, Hudson Swann. And the first thing I want is an explanation about why you decided to send Philo all the way to Ocean City to get us, when you could not come yourself.

Hudson denies it completely, but I cannot shake the feeling that as dumb as that dog is, he still managed to find Jeanne in Ocean City and get her to come back to Hudson, with the twins.

I guess Mr. Eddie is allergic to dogs.

Talking and Writing Good Oysterback:
A Foreigner's Guide
by Professor Shepherd

GETTING AROUND

Up the road: Could be anywhere from North Oysterback to Beijing; best not to ask, if you wish to appear *au courant*. Example: I'm goin' up the road, ya need anything?

Down the road: To Oysterback. Example: I gotta get down the road, now, my ice cream's about to melt.

Over to/down to/up to: Where you go when, and if, you get there. Examples: Over to Miss Nettie's, her crepe myrtles are in bloom. Down to the harbor, someone left a whole pile of almost new bushel baskets. Up to Salisbury, they had a drive-by shooting last night.

Get up and down with: To meet with someone; to network. Example: I been tryin' to get up and down with Beth Redmond for 'bout two weeks now over the Drive-In Living Nativity Pageant.

WHAT YOU DO WHEN YOU GET THERE

Seven-course meal: A six-pack of beer and a crab cake.

Gunning: What you do when you shoot waterfowl with a shotgun. Example: We are gonna get up four o'clock and go gunning over to Booger Birdsong's farm.

Shooting: Interestingly enough, applies to geese but to no other waterfowl. Also, dove or other upland bird hunting.

Hunting: When you go out after some deer.

Carrying a party: What an Oysterback boy does when he takes a bunch of foreigners gunning for money. (See "Just Plain Folks" below.)

Playing cards: Not advised for the foreigner. Tonk, a bastardized jailhouse form of gin, is always a good game to know.

Dredging/oystering/tonging: What you do when you go out in the boat to harvest bivalves. Examples: We was goin' oysterin' this mornin' but the water was all froze up. He went tonging with a pair of nippers and brought in 'bout a half [bushel]. *Note:* Never use the word *bushels* when describing the amount of an oyster harvest. "We got three, four" means three or four bushels of crabs or oysters. It is considered extremely rude to ask a waterman about the size of his catch, although a generally phrased question about harvest conditions can be acceptable after several minutes of idle conversation.

Crabbing: Harvesting crustaceans. Example: We was goin' crabbin' this morning, but it was blowing too much.

Party: (I) A verb. Example: Since we couldn't go crabbin', we partied down to the Blue Crab last night real late. (II) See "Just Plain Folks."

Running: Having an affair, usually with someone else's spouse. Example: Oh, she was runnin' Johnny Bob for 'bout six, seven months before Crystal found out.

Passing the time of day: General, pleasant conversation, with a touch of gossip, engaged in upon casual meetings in public places, such as a post office, a local store, a street, a bar, or church. Often engaged in between two automobiles on a two-lane blacktop. Passing the time of day is a strong Eastern Shore custom. Not to pass the time of day is considered a deep breech of etiquette, barring the most dire emergency circumstances, such as fire, childbirth, or the beginning of a softball game.

Baseball: A sacred ritual, taken very seriously.

Fishing: Another sacred ritual.

JUST PLAIN FOLKS

Native: Someone whose family has been in Oysterback since the beginning of God. Some Native American blood helps here. Example: The Swanns come over on the *Doxy;* they're natives from 'way back.

Local: From the West Hundred, although not necessarily from Oysterback. Example: Oh, the Buggs are local, they're from over to Patamoke, but Inez lived in Cambridge for twenty-six years.

Transplant: Someone who has moved to Oysterback and is tolerated, if not quite totally socially acceptable. Example: Sally and Bob are transplants; they use a mallet to eat crab claws.

Foreigner: A person from outside the West Hundred area (this could be anywhere from Bibble's Corner to Paris) who is so clueless, insensitive, and vulgar as to be beneath contempt. Example: That woman who wants to fill in all them wetlands over to Widgeon Marsh is a foreigner from Ohio somewhere, pay no mind.

White Christmas trash: Beneath contempt; the sort of people who have rusting pickup trucks in the front, not the back, yard. Example: If you didn't know Earl Don was from around here, you'd think he was white Christmas trash with all those crab pots in the living room.

Party: A plural noun. Usually, a group of urban men (foreigners) in expensive gear from Bean or Bauer who come to Oysterback to sit in a duckblind, talk dirty, and take a shot at a goose every now and then, led by a (local) guide who has mixed emotions about their male bonding sessions and has never read Robert Bly. Example: I had a whole party of doctors from Washington seaduckin' t'other day, talkin' some weird stuff about wild men and drums—they was nice guys but strange.

ODDS AND ENDS

Box: Dead oystershell and other debris.

Cull: Live, market-size oysters.

Stuffer: Stuffed goose used as decoy.

Picking it all over: Analyzing an event, person or thing at great length. Examples: Well, I just yearned for Helga Wallop to pick it all over with about Doreen Redmond's new miniskirt. Huddie and Junie picked it all over for a while then decided that Orville Orvall's redistricting plan was not much to write home about, because November wasn't that far away.

Up in the bed: Where you are on Saturday morning, when you have a cold, where you make love or watch David Letterman. Example: We were laying up in the bed about four-five in the morning when we heard the fire whistle go off and knew Mr. Eddie had set fire to the curtains again.

Tear a new hole: To do severe damage to someone. Example: She was so mad at him when she found out he was runnin' LaVerne, when Crystal got a hold of him, she tore him a new hole.

Come-to-Jesus: (I) Religious experience, as in John Wesley's Great Awakening. Example: When they had that revival preacher over to the Patamoke Church of the Holy Fire Baptized, Ferrus Buckett had a real come-to-Jesus that lasted about a whole week. (II) A serious altercation. Example: After Huddie Swann caught Paisley Redmond sucking the gas out of his boat, they had a come-to-Jesus over it.